GIVE + TAKE

GIVE + TAKE

stona fitch

Thomas Dunne Books ⚏ St. Martin's Press
New York

This is a work of fiction. All of the characters, organizations, and events portrayed in this novel are either products of the author's imagination or are used fictitiously.

THOMAS DUNNE BOOKS.
An imprint of St. Martin's Press.

MAY 2 4 2010

GIVE + TAKE. Copyright © 2008, 2010 by Stona Fitch. All rights reserved. Printed in the United States of America. For information, address St. Martin's Press, 175 Fifth Avenue, New York, N.Y. 10010.

www.thomasdunnebooks.com
www.stmartins.com

Library of Congress Cataloging-in-Publication Data

Fitch, Stona.
   Give + take / Stona Fitch.—1st ed.
       p. cm.
   ISBN 978-0-312-59987-4
   1. Jazz musicians—Fiction.   2. Thieves—Fiction.   3. Swindlers and swindling—Fiction.   4. Wealth—Fiction.   5. Satire.   I. Title.
II. Title: Give plus take.   III. Title: Give and take.
   PS3556.I816G58 2010
   813'.54—dc22

                                                                    2009045707

First published in the United States by Concord Free Press

First Thomas Dunne Books Edition: May 2010

10 9 8 7 6 5 4 3 2 1

For ann

Wrong is right.
—Thelonious Monk

cleveland

My fingers lower to the keys, as warm and familiar as skin. My ten-foot Bösendorfer languishes in a stranger's Noho loft, but I put that memory aside. It's just me and the slightly battered Baldwin tonight, two damaged nightclub veterans on a low stage, our world defined by a radiant ellipse from a flickering spotlight. Beyond it wait huddled lovers and clusters of bankers anxious to be entertained.

With its slow intro, *East of the Sun* always works as an opener. My fingers limber after a few bars, the audience disappears, and my mind floods with whatever chemical wave my brain releases when I'm at complete peace with the world. I could say more, but one man's bliss is another's boredom.

Tonight's set merges with the thousands I played along the rarified circuit of clubs and hotels from New York to San Francisco. For the next couple of hours, my left hand marks progressions of solid chords while my right traces the melody with smart embellishments—a straight-ahead style, listenable and marketable. Through Malcolm, my agent, a new club in the Flats has overpaid me to play three sets that will encourage people to buy more blue martinis, beer imported from Holland, and scallop appetizers on charred sugar-cane skewers.

I think of jazz the way a safecracker might; the right mix of familiar melodies and resonant chords sends tumblers clicking into place and opens long-locked doors. My time at the keyboard does more than relax and entertain the audience. Each song causes subtle emotional shifts, triggering spending, tips, and glowing online reviews that will bring others and their appetites and credit cards to the Buckeye Club.

When you carve the world down to its bones, you find money waiting in the marrow.

I lead the second set with *Parker's Mood* because the club owner asked me to and the general rule is to play a request unless it's a room-clearer. Or *Moondance.* At the beginning of *Evidence,* a clean little Monk number, I drop in new bass chords for eight measures. Not slop—diminished sevenths, some with the ninths worked in—fine subtle chords except they have nothing to do with the song I'm playing.

Couples nod away to the music, drinking at the faster pace appropriate for this time of night, on their way to having sex.

After all, the ultimate product we're selling is carnal. No fine-tuned ear perks up at dissonance in the bass. But a subtle warning to stop messing around beams from the Baldwin's smudged black cover. My conscience chimes in as well.

I know where stunts like this lead. Undone by dark rum and financial troubles, Jackie Morgan, one of Malcolm's best players, lost it about a year ago with a furious hour-long rethinking of *Kumbaya* that got him fired from the circuit for good and created a warning for the rest of us. *Bebop Kumbaya.*

My left hand comes back into line, finishing the chorus on time and in key, hanging on the dominant for a while and resolving. Applause.

I play a dozen songs in a trance—eyes half-closed, mind hovering over the melody like a lost summer cloud. There are worse lives.

The woman in the black blouse sits with some friends from work, their table an oenoscape of bottles and glasses. They discuss, laugh, stare. She watches my hands when I play, nodding gently in rhythm to *Willow Weep for Me,* the Art Tatum version. She holds her hand up to her throat as she listens, her fingers tracing along her collarbone.

By the end of the third set, her friends have left and only she remains—a freckled, strawberry-blond woman in her mid-thirties, attractive but kind of fierce. Blame a night of wine for inspiring her to wave me over to her table when my last set is finished and introduce herself. Jan tells me she just made vice president of investor relations, hence the night out with her friends from the bank.

"It's not the most interesting job in the world," she says.

"Certainly not as interesting as . . ." She stretches out a hand and plays air piano.

"You'd be surprised." I'm sure she has a piano in her apartment or suburban dream home. People like to own nice pianos. Some even play them.

It's almost 2 A.M. and the bartender is smashing empty beer bottles into a plastic trash bin. The lights blaze abruptly at bug-kill level.

"Drink up," Jan says.

"This wine isn't that good."

"I have some good red at my place," she offers, then, "and a piano."

Yes.

"A Steinway."

"Upright or grand?" I ask, as if that makes a difference.

"Grand. It's rosewood."

I rub my chin in faux contemplation. "I'd really like to play it."

She laughs. I pull on my suit coat and tuck a thick black binder under my arm. My fakebook goes everywhere with me, a jazz bible with all the apocrypha thrown in and some surprises at the back.

Jan grabs my shoulder as she stands up, wobbling on her heels for a moment. "You know, you're really funny," she says. "My friends thought you looked like you might be."

"I'm funny, all right."

A little charm and a sense of humor can take you places. Tonight it takes me spinning along Lakeshore Boulevard in Jan's Audi, which she handles like a pro. The interior smells of leather, coffee, and wine breath. She reaches over and gives my knee a confident squeeze to reassure me that everything is fine.

"I don't usually . . . you know," she says softly.

"Bring musicians home from nightclubs?" I say.

"Yes, that."

I smile. My appeal has little to do with looks. I expect nothing. I listen and pay attention, which makes me the antidote to most other men.

Jan's place is on the upper floor of a new apartment building in Lakewood. We kiss in the elevator, Jan pressing me back against the metal railing. The doors open and we stumble directly into the living room, the furniture all soft leather and chrome, track lighting set low. It looks out over other buildings, each glowing window an advertisement for *home*.

Jan wraps her arms around me from behind. "What're you looking at?"

"The lights," I say.

"An apartment building over there caught fire last summer." She points. "A bunch of people were killed. The ashes floated over here. The deck up on the roof was coated with them. It looked like snow." Jan shivers. "It was a terrible thing, that fire. A building just like this one. It could have been my ashes floating around. I don't want to think about it."

I nod.

"I'll get us a glass of wine. Cabernet?"

"That would be great." I sit at Jan's piano. In the stack of music there are beginner's books, a couple of dreaded Czerny manuals, a child's name scrawled on each—*Gwen,* Jan's daughter. The fragments of conversation at the club and since start to click into place. Jan is recently divorced. Joint custody of Gwen, husband has her on the weekends. Jan doesn't want to be lonely. And who can blame her? Not me.

I play *Embraceable You,* the Parker version, which swings a little more than most. The piano has a clear tone and good action. Jan pads across the parquet floor behind me and sets a glass of wine carefully on the piano. I stop playing and turn. She's backlit by track lighting, outlining her hair, down now, falling on her broad shoulders.

"Surprise," she whispers. Jan's naked, her long legs converging in darkness behind her hands, a nod to discretion.

It takes more than this to surprise me. I stand and we kiss slowly, then I run my fingers along her strong back, the shoulder blades held tight. The divorce, work—Jan's carrying it all around like a sack full of stones.

She's working on my belt but I slow her hand. Everyone is in such a hurry, pushing the tempo, rushing to resolve. I lower Jan onto the leather couch. Starting at her toes, I rub my fingers along her skin in circles, working her skin like clay.

"Strong hands." Jan edges toward me, letting a stranger's hands roam. Her feet merit at least five minutes, long enough to loosen each joint, but not so long that Jan begins to worry that I'm a creep with a fetish.

Her toe ring is of a snake eating its own tail. I run my finger around it. "An *ouroboros*."

"What?"

"Your ring's called an ouroboros. A symbol. Egyptian, I think. Something about the eternal cycle of birth and death."

"That's a depressing thought."

I look at her. "Seems okay to me."

"I just liked it because it was the only gold one they had at the store. Most toe rings are silver. The snake's eyes are diamond chips."

The tiny bits of diamond catch the light, compound it, send it back. They'll be glimmering long after Jan and I are bones in the ground, *a depressing thought,* as Jan might say. I move on, rub gentle circles along her ankles.

Jan is heavier in the arms, more splotched along the shoulders than acceptable in our retouched, hardened era. But she is beautiful, carrying a banked fire of soul and grace.

Jan's shinbones are hard as stone beneath my fingers as I press gently along her leg. A slow run up the inside of a thigh elicits a low sigh, better than any applause. She arches back into the leather, raises her hands above her to hold the chrome frame.

"I . . ."

I reach up and touch her lips and she licks my fingers. My fingertips run lightly along her narrow collarbone, the place she touched when we spoke back at the club, and find a hard bump just before the small hollow.

Jan freezes. "I broke it," she says quietly. "Or more accurately, my husband did. We were arguing and he pushed me down the stairs at the health club."

"I'm so sorry," I say. My parents' sullen fights were Gordian knots of accusations and recriminations. But broken bones are damage of a different sort.

I want to set Jan right with temporary repairs. It's my part of the bargain, the commodity I bring to the secret economy that we're creating here in her apartment in the lull between midnight and day.

The sky shifts to indigo, the stars wheel over Cleveland. Jan's skin gives beneath my touch. The snake eats its tail. We have hours to go. There are new melodies to play, complicated chords to resolve before we sleep.

I glide naked through the gray apartment, fakebook under my arm. Jan lies on the couch. She's covered with a blanket. Hours together have left Jan asleep and me covered with her scent, as if I'd submerged myself in a pool of Jan. Every inch of me is redolent of her, except the inches that you might be thinking about. Those remain dry and un-Janned—conventional conquest is not part of my repertoire anymore.

Take a moment and look at your hands. Imagine that your fingers are ten penises of different lengths and purposes. They are always hard; no need for Viagra. They are remarkably flexible and strong, working for hours without getting sore or turning smaller. They do not impregnate.

Good hands are the most important sexual organ. You heard it here first.

I peer into a room with stuffed animals on the bed and drawings on the wall. Down the hall, a glowing laptop screen lights Jan's office sickly blue. In the bedroom, I walk quickly to the dressing area, then pull a small metal kit from the hidden flap in the back of my fakebook. I take out a flashlight, flat as a credit card, click it on, and hold it between my teeth to guide me as I open each drawer with my knuckles. The top drawer is where people hide their pasts, tucked behind the socks and underwear.

Sure enough, there's a small red rayon pouch waiting in the back, and inside, Jan's gold wedding band and engagement ring. I twist a jeweler's magnifier into my eye and check the fundamentals. The engagement ring's diamond clocks in at close to two carats, cut in the *round brilliant* style, fifty-eight smooth facets all the way around. The color looks good, nice brilliance, no yellow or gray shading. Clarity is harder to check here in Jan's dim, airless dressing area. All diamonds have blemishes, fractures of varying degrees from when they were formed deep in the earth. Inclusions are hard to see but unique—the diamond's memory. Like Jan, her diamond has a few dark clouds, but nothing too terrible.

I open the metal kit and check the rows of boxes inside, glittering with stones of all shapes, sizes, and brightness. They're the best synthetic diamonds available, purchased by Malcolm from rogue diamond Jews. I pick the budget twin of Jan's diamond from its slot. Then I take out the reverse calipers and place them between the prongs of the setting. The steel ends in a soft bit of velvet, so they leave no mark as I apply a little pressure and Jan's ill-fated marital stone—a conflict diamond if there ever was one—tumbles into my hand.

I tuck the diamond under my tongue, a trick I learned a few years ago when a popular but sleepless New York talk show host almost caught me holding a handful of old-mine diamonds from her rivière necklace. I pop the new stone in and give the setting a small squeeze with the calipers to close it. Then I polish the ring with a pair of Jan's black silk underwear and put it back in its pouch.

I'm working very fast. The whole process of finding, stealing, and replacing the diamond takes less than a minute. Round, square, cushion-cut, new, old, large, small—I've handled more stones than a round-hatted Antwerp merchant.

Jan will probably never find out that her diamond is fake. Her untrained eye will never notice that her jewelry has experienced a major westward decimal shift tonight. If my nightwork is ever discovered, she'll probably blame her ex-husband. Maybe Gwen will discover it forty years from now when she's selling off Mom's jewelry. If the switch is discovered, Jan's homeowner's policy will pay for it, and few have a soft spot in their hearts for the insurance industry.

The real criminals are the diamond cartel, which manages to convince people like Jan and her brutish ex-husband that they need a diamond the size of a chickpea, then carefully controls production and supply to keep its value high. Diamonds are as common as bricks. I'm working to clear the landscape of over-valued, culturally loaded consumer items. I'm extracting value from private property and releasing it like a genie from a bottle.

It starts here, late at night in a stranger's apartment, when I search out the shine and fly away with it.

Weak light filters through the windows and tells me it's time to go downstairs and catch a cab back downtown to my hotel. I gather my black suit from the living room floor and pull it on, smooth the wrinkles with my hands, then lean down to kiss Jan on the forehead. She stirs slightly and smiles. Maybe our brief time together has left her happier and less burdened. At least that's what I hope as I walk toward the elevator.

Yes, I steal. I make no apologies for it. Stealing is unimportant. But what you do with the money makes all the difference in the world.

chicago

Fakebook tucked under my arm, I leave my room at the Drake and walk south. My uniform of choice—a long-sleeved white dress shirt and black flat-front pants, shiny German shoes—keeps me as invisible as a good waiter.

The morning light banks off the lake. Sidewalks are already heating up, shoppers laden. I know my way around the city. I was born and raised in Chicago, headquarters of Moore's Frozen Foods, Chief's employer as he led our family on its socioeconomic shakedown cruise from Glenview to Lake Forest. And I studied at the University of Chicago (major in economics, minor in nightclubs) for a couple of years before being distracted by *better opportunities,* as Malcolm would call them.

Along the retail lucreway of Michigan Avenue, I try not to appear too interested in the Cartier window display. In a few blocks I leave the steely heart of downtown and pass a deli, a shoeshine place, a couple of ancient taverns.

When I was a boy wandering through downtown, I saw every subtle shift of the sky, noticed every store, and remembered all the details. A deli in Old Town where all the waiters wore short ties to keep them out of the pastrami fat. The fast fingers of the dealers at the Marshall Field's stamp counter. The pieces of ancient buildings embedded in the base of the Tribune Tower.

I turn, searching for the right neighborhood. A few streets later, I stop opposite a low apartment building, yellow stucco with a brown entryway. A young mother hauling her infant daughter in an Indian-print sling walks out of the building and catches the bus. A few minutes later, an ancient woman shuffles out behind an aluminum walker, smokes a cigarette, then flicks the filter into the gutter before she walks back in.

The entryway turns quiet after a few minutes and I glide across the street. I walk like Miles Davis, cool but coiled, ready to unleash a hard knot of furious notes. This would be early Miles, before he turned his back on his audience and started hitting a clam every eight bars or so and calling it art. I know the perils of imitation, but Miles lets me move invisibly through neighborhoods by day, bedrooms by night.

The narrow vestibule smells of burnt onions. Flyers for takeout pizza and debt reduction litter the floor. The battered mailboxes of the Lakeview, forty-two in all, bear peeling tape and a United Nations roster of names. From the back of my fakebook I take out a thick stack of $100 bills and divvy them up. I've become adept at division. Everyone gets two, the occasional box with more names gets three.

The familiar euphoria washes over me like the Spirit descending or opiates crossing the blood-brain barrier. I've lingered in hundreds of entryways like this—eggy air, piss whiff, bare bulb shining, floor tiles cracked like a dried-out riverbed. Today everyone will find cash along with their bills. The stack dwindles and I push Ben Franklin into his final mailbox. The thrill is gone, replaced by an urgent need to get away quickly before the building super spots me.

Back at the Drake, I take the elevator downstairs to the Cape Cod Room, where I'll be playing a three-night stretch. In the glass case outside the club waits the press glossy of me in a dark suit, sitting at the keyboard of a gleaming Steinway. I'm staring off into the distance, hair black and shining, eyes inviting. Chief's family was English, Eileen's Czech, making me a standard Chicago-style mutt. My semi-mysterious look is calculated. After all, all musicians need to get over with an audience. We invent someone more exotic than we are and eventually that someone becomes us.

THREE NIGHTS ONLY. FROM NEW YORK. JAZZ SENSATION ROSS CLIFTON. I am not from New York, though Malcolm insists that we all say we are since it *classes us up*. I am not entirely sure what a jazz sensation is, but I know that I'm not one. And Malcolm decided long ago that Ross Wolfshead, my real name, was too scary and hard to say.

A new poster hangs next to mine. Another of Malcolm's travelers is playing here the week after me—Marianne London, a singer in a tight blue dress. Marianne has long reddish hair and a good smile. She's standing in the crook of a grand piano, unaccompanied, I notice. She seems too young and dewy to be on Malcolm's circuit and I decide to ask him about this Marianne London sometime, find out what the real story is behind the patently fake name and the innocent smile.

I knock on the door and a young pale man with a broom lets me in.

"Hey." Sweeper nods and identifies me as the entertainment rather than the guy delivering beer. Fleeting recognition is about as good as it gets.

"It's over there." He points into the main room, rustic and dimly lit with small tables covered with white tablecloths. The kitchen staff clatters away, getting ready for the lunch crowd. The air smells of chowder and bread. Near the bar waits an ebony Yamaha grand, its top down. I open it up, check to make sure the locks are on the wheels. Rolling the piano into people while they eat dinner is regarded as very unprofessional.

First I run up and down the whole keyboard in B major, almost all black notes, an out-of-kilter scale with tricky fingering in the left hand. I play a little sequence of chords that has been stuck in my head. I pound a quick, hard bass figure to check the lower register, find it's not bad, though a bit boomy. Then I add a few bars from an Ornette Coleman solo.

In all, I run the piano through its paces for about fifteen minutes. My work is done for now. But I keep playing. Nascent melodies cycle from my mind and out my fingertips—three notes from a cab horn this morning, the pattern of a conversation I heard through the hotel room wall last night, a song my mother used to sing when I was a kid, one about rolling a silver dollar across a dancehall floor. These hours of freedom at the piano are my reward for days spent in rental cars and hotel rooms.

On the road, I'm alone—no one to talk to, to call, to miss. But at the piano, I'm joined by Monk, Bill Evans, James P. Johnson, Delmar Robbins, and dozens of other companions from a genial guild of the fleet-fingered and dead. With stride bass and blistering runs, I hammer out the tedium of driving all day with public radio as my only companion. I forget the glacial lunches in small town cafés and the painful absence of anyone else who might share any beauty or insights gleaned from the road.

When I walk out of the Cape Cod Room hours later, my shirt is sweat-soaked, fingertips raw, mind purified by thousands of notes.

I spend the rest of the afternoon looking for a good health food store, finally finding one in Andersonville. Back at the Drake, I do some Tibetan exercises, eat hummus on whole-wheat pita bread, read the *Tribune*. Then I wash some clothes in the sink and shine my shoes. So much for the high life.

I customize my hotel room to my specifications. I remove all printed material—the triangular paper tents listing the movies, menus, guest guides, "Best of" city magazines—and stack it all neatly in the top desk drawer. I shove all of the furniture to the edges of the room, turn the television around and push it against the wall. I take the pillows off the bed and empty the minibar, replacing its miniatures of vodka and gin with carrot juice, organic apples, smoked tofu, pickled Japanese plums—the kind of food that Chief's beloved employer never got around to freezing. I unroll a small rug on the floor next to the window in a slanting rectangle of sunlight.

These changes exorcize the room of the anxious spirits of business travelers and subvert the hotel management's desire that I should spend every night watching overpriced pornography, drinking dinky trumpets of trouble, and making expensive phone calls. But more: now every hotel room I stay in seems like home, even if it's not.

Several years ago, I found that the road of excess did not lead to the palace of wisdom, as Blake promised. It led to the overpriced loft, a $75,000 Bösendorfer grand I couldn't play, an indigo blue BMW 7 Series sedan, and a temperature-controlled cellar full of wine I never drank. It led to a complicated girlfriend with whom I shared transactions instead of transcendence. It led to ulcers and migraines, self-induced misery at home and boredom at the keyboard.

It led to a new life and an economy of one.

I could spend all my nightwork earnings on psychoanalysis or meds, but why bother? As long as I'm stealing and giving money away, I'm happy enough. Call it therapy. Call it thievery. It works for me.

The sun passes high over the lake, the traffic coursing along Lake Shore Drive like shimmering blood cells along a crescent of vein. Chicago must have looked so modern to Chief and Eileen as they spun north in their Fairlane, driving straight from dusty Coffeyville with a screaming Ray in Eileen's lap, the nascent clot that would be me lodged in her uterine wall.

My family, leavened by promise and dreams, drove north to the second-largest American city. They were moving toward Chief's first real job and something else they could only vaguely articulate—toward *more*. They would buy a starter home, send their kids to college, take vacations in Florida. Their appliances would work. The food would be convenient. The sepia lives of their parents back in Kansas seemed desperate and sweaty. Their hard work would pay off someday.

Little did they know.

Though I get plenty of polite applause during my three nights playing the Cape Cod Room, I get no takers for my nightwork. Instead, I leave the Drake and take a walk past bars and empty parking lots, glowing hotel lobbies guarded by bellhops in absurd uniforms. I'm sure there are some great clubs along the quiet backstreets, but I have other plans.

I find a parking lot lit only by a dim streetlight. Parked in a reserved space far from the rabble of ordinary Toyotas and VWs waits a silver BMW 735i with a vanity plate that brags—OVER-QUOTA. It's not that different from the car I used to drive during my own failed period of conspicuous consumption. The owner wants to keep it safe from key scratches, drunken kicks. That's the problem with status symbols—other people secretly hate them.

I open my fakebook and pull on a pair of plastic gloves. The small blue and white plastic oval—the BMW Dealer Master Key, or DMK, as they're known in the trade—fits snugly in my palm. I take a quick look around, then walk to the BMW and press the silver button. I turn the DMK's small black dial slowly until the locks click and the alarm disables. The right frequency opens any door. Every BMW dealership has a DMK, which makes it easy for their top salesmen to work the lot, unlocking and starting new cars without fumbling for the right keys. When one shows up for sale Malcolm is quick to snap it up.

Inside, I put in the DMK and start the engine, then pull out slowly from the club parking lot. The BMW gives off the familiar hum of precision engineering.

The DMK brings a new elegance to car theft, which usually involves crowbars, broken glass, hot-wiring, and shrieking alarms. I hardly think of it as stealing; the cars are simply being reallocated.

I drive to the address on South Broadway that Malcolm e-mailed. He knows a BMW processor in every city. I check the rearview mirror; the road is almost empty.

At a light, a limousine pulls up next to me, a black Town Car, sleek and elegant. The driver glances at me then stares straight ahead, a small earpiece in his ear. In the back, through the gently tinted glass, I see a beautiful woman in a blue dress sitting next to an older man with gray hair. She smiles at something he says and I'm pretty sure I recognize Marianne London from her poster.

She looks my way and our eyes connect through the layers of glass, her skin lit by streetlights. But the light turns green and the limousine pulls out ahead of me, bound for downtown, leaving me in my stolen BMW, heading toward the southside.

The processor is located in a parking garage that looks closed for the night. I honk twice and the door opens. I pull in and the door closes. Three men in gray jumpsuits stride toward me as if I'm dropping the car off for an oil change.

"Nice one."

"Guess so." I shut off the engine and pop the hood.

They look at the engine, check the mileage. "Clean machine," one says. "You're in bonus territory."

"Sounds good."

One of the jumpsuits checks a list on a clipboard, looks up. "We're paying eight large for these today."

"Seems fair." I smile. It sounds like I've brought in a load of watermelons or cattle. I wonder for a moment what BMWs go for by the pound.

He hands me an envelope and I tuck it inside my fakebook without even checking. The processors are pros. Within hours, they'll have a buyer in Peking—a newly minted entrepreneur in need of automotive status—and make a hefty markup. I've been paid eight grand for ten minutes work. Tomorrow, this BMW sedan will be in pieces, packed up for its journey to China via container ship, joining the hidden global flow of illicit goods. In this transaction, only the BMW owner loses out, and my sympathy for him is minimal. His imposing silver sedan is definitely insured. And anyway, loss is part of the human experience.

The door buzzes and I'm on the street again.

I walk back toward the Drake. I pass another BMW parked on the street—a 3-Series this time—and press the DMK again, rotating the dial slowly just to hear the locks pop open. Then I lock the doors again. No need to push my luck.

Out on Lake Michigan, distant ships send out constellations of light. From my quiet hotel room, long past midnight, I watch the lake and wonder who's out on the water, where they're going. I can stare for hours: the shifting street reflections on the ceiling, afternoon sunlight raking down a wall, office windows at night, other evidence of everyday beauty.

I remember the limousine, wonder if Marianne London was riding in it. That two of Malcolm's players might find ourselves at the same stoplight at exactly the same time seems unlikely, but not impossible.

Malcolm is a legendary connector—collectors to paintings, dubious capital to suspect ventures, musicians to gigs. Elegant, cultured as a fin de siècle Viennese, painfully wry, Malcolm refers to himself as an *omniwhore,* willing to corrupt any market.

Once he ran an uptown art gallery, then a restaurant. Both closed under murky circumstances, Malcolm's favorite.

Now he unites the deft and daring to lucrative shadow careers, if they want them. Most musicians do. It's better than grinding along, broke and miserable. Malcolm helps us find something we can steal and convert to cash. Minus a 15 percent commission, of course. A saxophone player might specialize in check kiting. A drummer might take a second career removing art from museum walls or electronics from warehouses. Malcolm encourages us to be creative in our side projects. From what I know, I'm the only one on the circuit doing diamonds and BMWs. I wonder what Marianne London is up to.

The phone rings at four in the morning. I raise the receiver slowly.

"It's me." Ray never says more. My brother is convinced every phone is being monitored by Them. And with good reason.

"Up late or early?"

"Late. Been really busy. Jackson's getting a makeover."

"Again?"

"Always."

In the silence, I hear Ray's fast breathing. He walks into Montpelier to make calls—cell phones are too risky—and the trip winds him. He was never a fan of exercise of any sort except the fine-motor variety, our shared skill.

"It's April fifteenth. You still paying taxes?"

"Of course." Malcolm always keeps us on the level. A veneer of respectability can help you get away with a lot.

"Sucker."

"You make your choices, I'll make mine." Ray brings out a

testy side of me that I don't like. Though he would be loath to admit it, Ray has adopted some of Chief's bullying ways.

"Still tickling the ivories?"

I roll my eyes. "Yes." Ray knows nothing of my hidden work, though he introduced me to Malcolm years ago, setting my whole shadow career in motion. I don't trust Ray to keep a secret, though he's the most secretive person I know. His barn outside Montpelier houses a state-of-the-art computing infrastructure and a massive Heidelberg press. He's difficult, divorced with one son, and committed only to his work. But beyond that, he's like a stranger who happens to be my brother.

"I'm thinking of getting completely off the grid," he says softly.

"You've been saying that for a long time now." I haven't seen Ray in years, but I picture him bearded and keg-shaped, because I know he eats anything put in front of him.

He grumbles. "This time I mean it. I'm putting together a solar-powered generator."

I laugh.

"Shut the fuck up!" he shouts.

"I'm not laughing at you."

Silence. More rasping.

"Listen, bro. I need a favor."

"Not a loan, I'm guessing."

Even Ray has to laugh at that. "No, I need to send the kid to you for a couple of weeks. I really have to focus."

I shake my head. "No. Way." The kid is my nephew, Cray.

"I don't care what the fuck you say, I'm sending him."

"Isn't he supposed to be in school?"

"He's homeschooled."

"I bet." I think of the Artful Dodger schooling Oliver Twist.

"He needs to get around a little. It's been a long fucking winter."

"*No*. And I mean it this time." Two years ago, Cray traveled around with me for a disastrous week.

"He's changed. He's grown up now. Got his license. I know! He can drive you around."

"The last thing I need is a chauffeur."

"Then he can carry your bags or something."

"No." Cray put a serious crimp in my nightwork and I wasn't in the mood to babysit him again.

Ray pauses. "Look, he's sixteen now. And he's trying to figure out where he's going with his life. I thought it might do him some good to get out on the road. Don't you think?"

I say nothing.

"You're playing in Dallas next month, right? He'll meet you."

I pause. "How do you know where I'm staying?"

"You always stay at the same hotel. You're really predictable, bro. I know everything there is to know about you."

"No, you don't."

"Yes, I do." Our boyhood echoes across the years.

"All I'm saying, Ray, is don't send him out to see me. Repeat. I do not have the patience to deal with Cray."

Ray pretends not to hear. "Be looking for him. He's taller now and he's got his hair dyed kind of a deep yellow . . . you'll see."

"Thanks for the update on my nephew. Don't send him."

"Don't tell me what to do."

The phone clicks and my brother is gone.

Ray and I became playground grifters when I was in sixth grade and he was in eighth. Our classmates did little but play desk hockey with sticks they made from pencils, wire, and masking tape. Outsiders already, we were rarely invited to play and when we were, we were soundly beaten, since our opponents spent every idle minute at school slapping wads of tape across their desks.

Wandering around the playground one afternoon, I found a half-empty tube of congealed tar left behind by workmen who had repaired the school's flat roof. The day was cold and raw and when I kicked the end of the tube, the tar cracked into shards on the ground.

"*Black opals,*" Ray whispered from behind me, then set out his plan. "Give me a handful and throw the rest into that Dumpster next to the gym. Whatever you do, don't tell anyone about it."

I nodded.

"In two weeks, we'll have a couple hundred dollars. Guaranteed."

"No way."

Ray smiled. "Yes way. But you have to help me."

I nodded, locked into the role of younger brother.

"Got any cash?"

I shook my head. Ray scowled. He ran a thriving candy and cigarette concession from his locker and always had money. He took out his wallet and handed me some dollars. "Put these in your pocket."

Back among the table-hockey players, Ray pretended to admire his black opal. I took a careful look at it and we improvised a bit of dialogue, shouted, pushed each other—all free advertising. Once we had a crowd, Ray went into his pitch. He was already a pro and soon the asking price for this rare black opal dug from the Chicago dirt was up to ten dollars. I chimed in with twelve dollars and waved my cash at Ray when he gave me the signal. Another slack-jaw shoved a twenty at Ray and he shook his head.

"Not for sale," he said. "I like it too much." He was building demand, customer awareness, market pressure.

For days, the entire school searched for black opals, which Ray claimed came from a deep vein of semiprecious stones somewhere beyond the basketball court. Kids scraped sticks along the hard ground during recess. They rushed back to the schoolyard after dinner and dug with shovels, using flashlights when darkness fell. None of the preteen prospectors came up with a black opal. We had the market cornered. Ray took on the confident, peaceful look of someone with an enviable and insurmountable competitive advantage.

A week later, Ray announced he would sell his black opal to the highest bidder after school on Friday. By the time our frenzied auction ended, he had two hundred and seventy-five damp, wrinkled one-dollar bills in his backpack. A group of fourth-graders had pooled their allowances and yardwork earnings to buy Ray's chunk of worthless tar.

Ray had plans for that cash. He wanted to buy a 1950-D Jefferson nickel, the rare one that would complete his collection. But the principal came for a visit that night. Chief uncovered our loot in Ray's backpack, and assumed that—as the fourth-graders claimed—we had stolen their hard-earned allowances. We were expelled. We spent that night huddled in our room, awaiting our punishment with a mix of fear and pride.

The devious work of the Wolfshead Boys had just begun.

Too rattled to sleep now, I sit in front of the hotel room window, watching the lights of the city. Somewhere along the horizon waits the Glenview bungalow where Chief started his way up the ladder at Moore's, where Eileen nurtured her greenhouse of grudges, where Ray and I began to lie, cheat, and steal.

I'm ready to leave the city of Chicago, so freighted with commodities, memories.

st. louis

A few miles southwest of Kankakee, I turn off the highway and drive down straight county roads bordered by cornfields that race by in a pale green blur. After a few minutes, I pull over and roll down my window, turn off the car. The engine ticks for a moment, then goes silent. A cloud of dust sweeps past and the air clears. I'm parked on a low rise that presides over impossibly straight and endless rows of corn. Anyone wanting to contemplate infinity need only stand at the edge of an Illinois cornfield.

As I open the car door urgent bells sound, reminding me, a

car thief, that I have left the keys in the ignition. I walk for a few minutes, then kneel by the side of the road and watch the red sun hover over the fields. Red-winged blackbirds fly low to rattle the corn. Down the verdant slope, a tiny dog runs figure eights behind a white farmhouse, laundry waving in a gentle breeze as if the world is exhaling.

The ground next to me is pale red and dry. I take a packet of diamonds from my pocket and drop them on the dirt. I took them during night visits across the country. But they're all less than a half-carat and flawed. They still glimmer beautifully in the late-afternoon sun, but they're nearly as worthless as Ray's black opals. I push them down into the ground, the day's warmth enveloping my hands.

I've been burying these dinky orphan diamonds all over the country, after decades on fingers, around wrists or necks. It seems right to me. I'm putting evidence where no one will find it and repatriating them to the earth. But I can see how someone might find it strange. I would have a few years ago.

Hands in the earth, eyes on the sun's slow descent, the beauty of the world lowers around me like a stage curtain of indigo and silver.

A bright light beams from behind me and boots scrape along the road. The day has faded and the dust around my hands is cold. I turn and squint into a blinding light. How long have I been lost here next to the fields?

"Please stand," a voice calls. "Now."

I pull my hands from the dust and rise slowly.

"Who are you?"

"Ross Clifton."

A beam of light moves from my eyes and across my dark pants, my shoes marked with dust, then trails along the ground between us. I can make out a dark figure, the glint of a silver belt buckle. In the distance, a low blue Illinois State Police sedan waits. So much for radiant moments.

"What are you doing here, Mr. Clifton?"

"I was driving from Chicago, stopped to rest for a few minutes."

"You were sitting there for over an hour. Neighbors reported you, thought you might be having a heart attack or some kinda problem. Were you?"

"No, of course not."

"Are you taking any medication, Mr. Clifton?"

I shake my head. "I haven't taken anything for years."

"Had anything to drink?"

"No."

"Then do you mind telling me what exactly were you doing over there in the dirt?"

Reburying stolen diamonds might not be considered a good answer. "I play the piano," I say. "I have a little arthritis in my hands. Sometimes keeping them in the dirt helps. It's warm."

"Am I supposed to believe that bullshit?" The policeman moves closer and I see he is young, a straight-backed black man with one hand holding his flashlight, the other on the handle of his service revolver. "I'm going to ask you to take out your wallet with one hand and toss it toward me."

"I don't carry a wallet."

"Where's your license?"

"In my jacket pocket."

"Then hand it to me."

I find my license and offer it politely. The patrolman shines his flashlight on it.

"New York. Long way from home, eh? And it says here your name's Ross Wolfshead, not Clifton. What kinda messed-up name is that?"

"That's my real name. It's English, my father's family name. Ross Clifton is my stage name."

A pause, as the patrolman tries to put this whole tableau in context—a skinny white musician, squatting in the dirt near a cornfield, crazy apparently.

"What kind of music do you play?"

"Jazz. Just played a few nights at the Drake in Chicago. I'm playing St. Louis tomorrow night. Then Kansas City."

"You get around then, do you?"

"I guess you could say that. I'm on the road a lot." Sweat starts to trickle down my sides. I definitely don't want the patrolman digging in the dirt or rummaging through my car.

Another pause. "Must be interesting."

I shrug. "Probably not as interesting as being a state trooper."

"Half the time I'm driving around, the other I'm doing paperwork." A long pause. "Weekends though, I play bass in a little trio."

"Electric or upright?"

"Electric."

"What kind of music?"

"Fringe stuff."

"Here in the heartland? Isn't that illegal?"

The patrolman laughs, hands me back my license. With that lame line, I'm in.

"Not illegal, just not very popular," he says. "You like Brother Jack McDuff?"

I smile at such an odd question asked in the twilight by a man with a gun. "Sure. I know a couple of his songs. *Do It Now*—that's got a tricky little bass part."

"I can't believe it. We just picked that one up."

"Hard four bars at the end, aren't there?"

"You're good, man. What are you, some kind of jazz master?"

"Hardly."

"We do *Snap Back Jack* too," he says, excited now.

I nod. "If you like McDuff, you'd probably like Mulgrew Miller." I actually don't know much about either. Jazz is baseball for indoorsmen, the kind who still hang out in clubs, listen to expensive Japanese CDs of bootleg Bill Evans outtakes. You pick your team—stride, swing, bebop, hard bop, West Coast cool, Afro-Cuban, fusion, acid jazz—and stick with it.

"Don't know that I've heard of him."

"Check out *Neither Here Nor There*—a nice fast little number. *Hand in Hand* is good too. More of a Latin feel to it."

We walk back toward our cars, glowing slightly in the last light.

"You play any Monk?"

"One of my favorites," I say. "Definitely in the top four. Monk, Parker, Miles, Mose." I don't bother mentioning James P. Johnson—hardly anyone remembers him.

"Old school, eh?"

"You could say that."

"Can't get our piano player to do Monk except the easy ones."

"Try *Monk's Mood* for starters. Hold on, I've got it here somewhere." We walk back to the car and I lean in to lift my fakebook from the seat. It falls open to the pouch of glimmering diamonds.

"You sure you don't need them?" The cop is right next to me, shining his flashlight in. I flip to the front quickly, rip out the right charts, and hand them over. I shrug. "If I don't know that song by now, I'm never going to learn it."

"Thanks. You go knock 'em dead in St. Louis."

"I will. I'll do that." I smile, then let it fade as I climb back into the rental car.

The patrolman waves. I wave back. Two musicians passing in the night.

Almost everyone is a musician. A hotel clerk who plays blues harmonica in the elevator shaft, a guitarist working at a coffee shop, a drummer lying on a Lower East Side corner selling records on a blanket. They're all musicians, part of the universal union able to carry a tune, remember some lyrics, put the notes together into a melody, and get across with an audience.

Songs return us to where we heard them first. They connect us to the people who wrote them, who played them before us, listened to them. Some nights I look out into the audience and see dozens of people, eyes lost in the middle distance, traveling back down a path. I'm just lighting the way.

I took piano lessons from a psychotic German named Mrs. Bernecasstler, who drilled me so incessantly that my fingertips hurt and I wanted to quit. She kept a collection of miniature plastic busts of composers in a box next to her. When I played poorly, she would rummage for the right composer, then hold him up and scream, *"Vhat are you trying to do to me!"*

Then I discovered James P. Johnson.

When I was fourteen, Chief jumped to a new level of management at Moore's and he enrolled us in the Kenilworth Hill

School, where Ray and I wore white shirts, monogrammed blazers, rep ties slung around our necks—and became unlikely little dandies with plans for everybody.

Kenilworth had a fancy media center with low pods of cubicles equipped with turntables, tape decks, and enormous headphones. Ray found that if you pulled out the headphone jack and stuck in a steel Parker pen, you could deafen everyone in your pod. I found an enormous record library stocked with jazz albums—Sidney Bechet, Jimmie Lunceford, Jelly Roll Morton, Jack Teagarden, Glen Gray, Joe Venuti.

On the morning I discovered my true calling, I huddled in a cubicle that smelled of hot wiring, vinyl, and mildewed album covers. I put an early James P. Johnson side on the turntable, *You've Got to be Modernistic.* Even before the intro was over, every hair had stood up on the backs of my arms as if blown there by a gust of prairie wind. A latter-day Liszt, a Harlem savant who never got his due, Johnson played so well it seemed physically impossible—right hand like a sledge, left like a hummingbird.

As I pressed the headphones tightly over my ears, I heard something more than a transcendent stride tune, thousands of notes cascading down like water. I heard optimism, the promise that no matter how bad times were, there would always be escape in music, grace, and sheer audacity. I listened to James P. Johnson over and over until my ears turned hot beneath the headphones.

Chief was working hard for some vague payoff that would justify all the overtime, meetings, office politics, and seething dinners with Eileen. We would buy a boat and cruise around Lake Michigan, Chief at the helm. Our family would live in a big house in Lake Forest, go to fine restaurants, vacation in London to search out our Wolfshead relatives and impress them with our new American money.

I didn't want any of it. All I wanted was to play piano like James P. Johnson. Nothing else mattered.

While I was exploring the intricacies of Harlem stride, Ray invented the *dickel,* a dime and a nickel sanded down and soldered together down in Chief's basement shop. Ray sold them to rich kids at school; they were all coin collectors. They knew that mint errors like this—freaks, they're called—were valuable, certainly worth more than the five dollars Ray charged. By the time they figured out the scam, Ray had pocketed a couple hundred bucks and moved on to two-headed quarters, pennies etched with Lincoln smoking a fat joint.

Ray had found exactly what he was going to do with his life too.

The Westin lounge looks out upon the iconic Gateway Arch, which, like most celebrities, looks smaller in real life. I play my usual first set to a good, crowded room. A bald guy tips me a twenty and requests *Our Love Is Here to Stay.* Deep into the second set, I stray far outside the melody of *East of the Sun* and the hotel guests applaud when I bring it back into line after eight bars. Make it sound risky and they'll cheer.

I play a set of moon songs—*How High the Moon,* then *Old Devil Moon* in the Mose Allison style. I skip *Moondance*—perhaps the most requested song in history—because it just isn't jazz, it has the word *fantabulous* in the second line, and I worry that if I play it, my next number might be *Bebop Kumbaya.*

Between the second and third sets, a woman sitting alone at the front table watches me as if trying to memorize my every feature. She's got short black hair cut in brutal bangs, her watery skin set off by a sparkling black dress.

Two hours later, the staring woman and I are horizontal in the Chairman's Suite, an enormous room high up in the Westin, so big that it has an entire dining room and living room as well as the elegant bedroom where she kisses me hard. Carla tastes of minibar Scotch and cigarettes. In a dispassionate flurry, she gathers my rumpled suitcoat from the bed and opens the door to a massive armoire and hangs my jacket among a careful row of dark suits.

"Always travel with a dozen Armani suits?"

"Very funny," Carla says. "They're my stupid husband's." Women who find themselves alone with a traveling musician after midnight rarely have anything good to say about their husbands or boyfriends.

"Will he be coming back soon to put them on?"

"Don't worry, he's meeting me here tomorrow. Flying in from New York. And what do you care, piano man? You saw I was married the moment we met." Carla sits back down on the bedspread and reaches out to touch my chest as she issues a liquor-fueled non sequitur. "You're not very hairy at all."

"No, I'm not," I say. "And I didn't know you were married."

"Didn't you see my wedding ring?"

I definitely notice rings. "You weren't wearing one."

"I guess I left it in the bathroom." She shrugs. "The engagement ring's a bit too much sometimes."

I perk up at the news.

"We married a few years ago—a marriage of convenience. Ryan gets convenient use of my money. I get convenient use of his corporate jet." She smiles at her own tired wit, cracks open another plastic nip of Scotch and offers it to me, then drinks it all herself.

If I ever needed proof that money doesn't make people happy, it's sprawled on the bedspread next to me.

"Are we going to do it?" Carla says. "Or did my husband's nice suits scare you off?"

"I'm not scared," I say. "But we're not going to do it the way you're used to."

Her green eyes flare for a second. "Ohh . . . something special planned?" She pulls off her black silk panties and drops them on the floor, unsnaps her bra. Even in the dim light of the bedroom, I can see that Carla's had some work done. She's forty-five with the breasts of a cheerleader. Her eyes are too defined, hair too dark.

"Sit for a moment," I say.

"Sit?" she says. "I don't want to sit. If you can't get it up, I have some Viagra. Do you need a Viagra, piano man?"

"No," I say.

"I said I want to fuck, not sit," she shouts.

"We can do both." I climb off the bed and sit in a straight-backed chair, hotel-issue Baroque, carved with eagles with arrows in their beaks. I wave Carla over and she slides off the bed, walks with a slight sway across the carpet. Her pubic hair is trimmed into a porny vertical swath, like an exclamation without the point. She turns around and presents her surgically sculpted ass to me, lowers it slowly as if I'm a piece of furniture. To her, I might as well be.

I turn her around gently and sit her on my knees, her legs around mine, feet barely touching the floor. I start by looking into her eyes. I trace her eyebrows with my index fingers, pressing gently against the low rise where they have been so carefully painted and plucked.

"Jesus that feels good . . ."

"Try to be quiet," I say, and go from eyebrow to cheekbone to earlobe, the innocent venues no one ever explores.

Ten minutes later, Carla's in a half-trance. I raise her up slightly by flexing my legs and pushing her up on my knees. She rises effortlessly, like the floating woman in a magic show. I lick the fingertips of my right hand and press them together in a narrow pyramid. I reach down and place this pyramid on the seat of the chair, then lower Carla down on it in increments so narrow that at first she doesn't even feel my fingers inching inside her.

"Oh my God." Her eyes pinch closed.

I turn my hand slowly clockwise, then back.

Carla reaches for the chair and tries to pull herself down but I push her back up with my legs, withholding any stolen increments. She has to wait, for once.

An hour later, I'm in the bathroom, flashlight clenched between my teeth, magnifier in my eye, looking at one of the largest diamonds I've ever seen. Carla was right. At almost four carats, the engagement ring really is embarrassing. I check the cut, find that it's okay. Inside the crown there are dozens of inclusions, black bits of unprocessed carbon like tiny cancers. Carla's diamond is impressive on the surface but shallow and flawed on closer inspection. Even so, it's worth plenty. One of the many ironies of diamonds is that the large ones can bully through any number of flaws. Small diamonds have to be perfect.

A single pull of the calipers extracts the diamond from its gaudy, platinum setting. I look at my face for a moment in the mirror, the low light of the bathroom shadowing the hollows of my cheeks, my dark eyes. My face looks more honest the more I steal.

Feeling triumphant, I flip Carla's diamond toward the ceiling with my thumb, open my mouth, and catch it like a grape. Except that it slips down my throat, and a grape doesn't have sharp facets.

I gag, then grab both sides of the sink and make a desperate, feral choking sound. My face reddens and my hands are shaking on the sink as I retch again, raising nothing, lodging the diamond even further in its esophageal setting.

The bathroom door opens and Carla wanders in, sits on the toilet, and unleashes a torrent of piss. She squints up at me. "My God, what did you do to me? I can hardly walk," she whispers.

I nod, try to pretend that I'm fine, then gag again, sending a recoil through my whole body.

"Feeling okay, piano man?"

I shake my head.

"Must be something you ate." She stands and rubs my back gently.

My eyelids lower slightly and the room grows dark at the edges.

"Once I ate a bad scallop—are you allergic to scallops, maybe?—and I woke up in the ICU with a plastic tube down my throat."

My whole body shakes, out of control.

Carla's at the vanity mirror, rubbing some kind of cream under her eyes. "Maybe you're allergic to nuts, everyone seems to be. Can you imagine that anything so innocent as a peanut could be . . ."

I press forward quickly to ram my stomach against the white corner of the sink. A hot gasp blows out of my mouth, and along with it, Carla's diamond. It ricochets off the tiles with a tiny click.

"Better?"

I gasp, run the water, splash it on my face. "Yes, much better," I say in a moment. "Choked on some water."

Carla shakes her head. "Got to watch that stuff. I try to stick with Bordeaux or single malt." She smiles and puts her arms around me, presses her cheek into my chest. "I feel so . . . incredible. I've never . . ."

I lay my fingers over her lips.

She nods. "I know, better not to talk about it. I won't say another word." She mimes locking her mouth and throwing away the little key. "Come back to bed. And bring those hands of yours."

I nod.

Carla drifts back into the bedroom.

I close the door with a click and retrieve my flashlight from the top of the medicine cabinet. I get down on all fours and crawl through the bathroom like a pig looking for a four-carat truffle. Not in the corner, not in the bathtub. I crawl toward the sink and peer underneath. Nothing. I look over the rim of the toilet and spot a glimmer at the bottom of the bowl beneath Carla's tea-colored pee and shrouds of toilet paper.

For someone who prides himself on being a complete professional, both onstage and during my nightwork, this particular evening is the equivalent of forgetting a song and hammering at the keyboard with lobster claws.

I swallow my pride, hoping it goes down a bit easier than Carla's diamond, and remind myself that urine is pure, that yogis drink it. Then I plunge my hand down into the piss and catch the stone between my fingers, the last act in tonight's performance finally over.

Like Carla, I used to have too much money, and it led me astray. It started with a simple desire—a better piano to replace my tinny upright. For years, I had dreamed of owning a grand piano. More specifically, I wanted, coveted even, a Bösendorfer, arguably the best piano in the world, and the most expensive. Alta, my girlfriend, encouraged me to buy myself one. I worked hard, I deserved the best, and anyway, it was a business expense.

Alta's work made her finely calibrated to appreciate timeless beauty and the objects that embodied it. She specialized in designing *Eames-era interiors,* which meant anything sleek, modern, and expensive, from what I could tell. Tall and serious, half-French, with long straight hair and unshakable poise, Alta made her clients feel okay about buying a German Expressionist print, a Mission desk, or beautiful knickknacks that cost five or six figures. That I loved her deeply made me ignore any worries I might have that I was straying disturbingly close to the ways of Chief, who believed that big-ticket purchases had medicinal properties.

I gathered up $75,000 in converted diamonds and BMWs, called headquarters in Vienna, and placed my order, sweat coursing down my sides. Instead of healed, I felt terrified.

Soon after, we realized that the living room of my apartment on University Place wouldn't hold a ten-foot grand piano. Actually, it would hold the piano, but little else.

But Alta and I had spotted a loft for sale on Bond Street a few months ago. We'd find ourselves wandering past it after dinner, gazing up at its row of original windows, the intricate gray-flecked marble details. *Bond Street*—its very name promised to bring us together forever. Alta turned reverent when we talked about buying the loft during long walks, phone calls from the road, or afternoons in my cramped apartment, which seemed to shrink palpably.

Bond Street. I bought the loft and we moved in together—two decisions tied together with a bright green ribbon of money. Malcolm negotiated a deal with the owner, a once-plush financial services guy anxious to unload it. I made the down payment in cash.

At first, change, space, and more time together brought us happiness. When I think of those first few months together, a strong hand squeezes some unnamed and imaginary gland that secretes sadness—one found somewhere just below my heart.

Then Alta decided that she needed a cat to keep her company when I was on the road. We bought a kitten in Soho and named her Sake, Alta's drink of choice. Sake was a Savannah, a rare, half-wild breed with short gray hair who stalked along the high-gloss floors like a pocket-sized panther. She cost $3,000 and some change.

Alta also thought our loft needed new furniture. Three months and $60,000 later, we had a set of original black leather Barcelona chairs, floor-to-ceiling custom bookshelves, a Ligne Roset bedroom set, and vintage Nichols rugs. Each purchase seemed to trigger late-night discussions of what to buy, where to find it, how it might fit with everything else. Alta carried a vague dissatisfaction with her, as if forever hunting for one last, perfect missing piece of our life.

The first sign of trouble came from Sake, who started to eat pencil erasers, rubber bands, food wrappers, and other colon-clogging plastic debris. One night, while Alta and I were out having dinner in Tribeca, Sake destroyed the Barcelona chairs, shredding the leather to get to some kind of midcentury adhesive that she craved like a kitty crackhead. When we came home, Alta crumpled to the floor and cried for hours in the fetal position.

Several thousand dollars in vets and feline psychiatrists later, Sake was diagnosed with *feline pica,* a nervous disorder that would require regular counseling and constant vigilance. We had to get rid of anything she could chew.

Then finally, the Bösendorfer arrived one June Saturday, hoisted in through the front windows of the loft. A crowd gathered to watch the enormous piano hovering like a black Austrian cloud over Bond Street. I directed it into the living room, placed it in the corner out of the sun. Sake used the opportunity to devour a Styrofoam coffee cup one of the piano movers left on the floor.

When the movers had finally left, I sat at the infinitely adjustable, ergodynamic bench ($2,500). I put my fingers on the keyboard and felt its cool elegance. It was Christmas in June. My payoff had come.

I played a James P. Johnson number first, *Carolina Shout,* then *Monk's Straight, No Chaser.* The piano was responsive and fast. The whole room seemed to vibrate when I played most of *All Blues,* adding an extra sixteen-bar solo. Alta sat next to me on the bench, smiling, listening more intently than she ever had before.

Midway through *Brilliant Corners,* the phone rang. It was the woman who lived in the loft downstairs, May d'Assiandro. I had never met May, though I had heard she was an artist and that she had been in the Whitney Biennial a few years earlier. She specialized in gnawing plastic doll heads, something Sake would have been glad to help her with, I'm sure. From what Alta could decipher through the screaming and crying, May was hypersensitive to sound, particularly the sound of the piano, which reminded her of "something bad about to happen." Alta said we'd keep it quiet and hung up.

Back at the Bösendorfer, I touched the keys as lightly as possible, playing an almost inaudible version of *Almost Blue.* The phone rang again immediately. Sake skidded into the living room and began to projectile-retch Styrofoam.

A few weeks later, we heard from May d'Assiandro's lawyers; she was suing us for "sonic disturbances contributing to an inability to function as a working artist." Then Sake ate the keys off the lower register of the Bösendorfer.

I was in hell, one of my own making, the worst kind. I had a piano I couldn't play, a loft that served as a high-priced prison/furniture showroom, and a cat that spewed plastic.

The disintegration of our loft paralleled our own. Like so many other fools in love, Alta and I had equated prime real estate with the promise of domestic happiness. I'll skip the next few months of our dwindling love affair, rife with simmering regret, slammed doors, and arctic silences—a back avenue of love rarely explored in song, and for good reason. When Alta finally moved out and took a job in San Francisco, I was numb with sadness. Less so when Sake went to a feline rehabilitation clinic upstate.

When you're in hell, there's only one real road out—repentance. Mine was financial. I sold the loft at a loss to a younger financial services guy, who kept the Bösendorfer, *for looks,* as he put it so eloquently. I rented a room in an apartment building on Elizabeth Street, a kind of clubhouse where Malcolm let his musicians stay for low rent.

I knew that no matter what I bought with my diamond and BMW money, it would be tainted. Some people give up drugs or drinking. I gave up money. I began my new life out on the road, stealing and giving away, staying in constant motion like a long run of sixteenth notes.

I would keep my damaged heart to myself and put my fast hands to good use.

I pay my twenty-dollar cover just like everyone else and take the table in the very back of the Infoscape Jazz Lounge at the Ambassador Hotel. Thanks to the club's corporate sponsor, every table has free Wi-Fi, which keeps half of every couple pecking away on various handheld devices. Not exactly behavior that makes for friendliness, but that's fine with me. I'm not here to talk to anyone.

Two glasses of warm red wine later, Marianne London takes the stage, nodding and smiling to the crowd, which applauds wildly. Her gentle reddish curls fall on her bare shoulders. Her carefully revealing black dress and her simple strand of three diamonds on a thin gold chain urge me to dismiss her as nightclub eye candy. But I'm impressed at how she's won over the crowd before she even opens her mouth.

Then her pianist hits the bass intro to *You Don't Know What Love Is,* a risky melancholy opener, and Marianne sings. Her voice is pure and strong but seductive, more Sarah Vaughn than Billie Holiday, more Kansas City than New York. She's old school, not trying to sound like Diana Krall or her ilk, voices as silken and perfect as their hair. Summing up a voice is like describing a wine—much is lost in translation from experience to words. All I can say is that by the third verse, the one about not knowing how a lost heart feels, I'm completely hooked.

Marianne stalks the front of the stage during *Taking a Chance on Love,* using the long chorus to scan the audience and connect her gaze with dozens of men. I have to smile. It's like watching my sultry twin in action. Except with one big difference. All I can do is send out looks from behind the keyboard. Untethered from the piano, she's in close with the crowd, a beautiful wolverine among graying sheep.

During *I Don't Know Enough About You* she takes it even further, walking between tables and laying her hand on the shoulders of dozens of men like a faith healer. Those sitting with their wives or girlfriends try to feign indifference. But their gleaming eyes give them away; they love being singled out.

Then suddenly, she's coming toward me, singing the verse about knowing a little about biology, psychology, and geology. I have to laugh at that one—I know a thing or two about geology too, at least the gemstone part of it.

As she moves closer, the oxygen in the room seems to double and I think she's singing just for me, even though of all people, I ought to be immune to any strain of musical seduction by now. But still, my heart is racing, even more when she pauses in front of me, puts her hands on my shoulders, and stares right in my eyes as she sings. The follow spot catches us as she's finishing the chorus—*But I don't know enough about you.* Then she winks at me, as if we're both in on the game she's playing, as if this line actually means something. Then she trails her fingers across my shoulders and moves through the crowd for the next verse. The spotlight trails her and abandons me to darkness.

All through the dim club, ardent fans are reinventing Marianne London. She's a blank screen and they're a hundred flickering projectors beaming conflicting story lines.

Marianne is mysterious. She's blunt and direct.

Marianne's an intellectual. She's never read a book.

Marianne is easy to get along with. She's a wildcat.

To me, Marianne is another long-suffering traveler trapped on Malcolm's endless circuit. She's looking for a way out, someone to steal her away from her admirers. She's sick of singing alone and annoyed at her light-handed accompanist. Clearly she's waiting for the right piano player to come along. Someone who understands, who listens. Someone a lot like me.

I leave the table and walk out of the club before she finishes the song, not wanting to share my version of Marianne with anyone. I can still hear her beautiful voice a block away.

kansas city

Riley's is a new club packed with businessmen. They're talking, drinking martinis, occasionally looking up when I play a particularly fast bit in a reworked version of Charlie Parker's *A Night in Tunisia,* a song I learned when I was thirteen. Parker is a native son—there's an enormous blue sculpture of his head at 18th and Vine. There's the Jazz Museum and plenty of clubs.

But my audience disappoints me. I blame it on meat. The crowd has eaten too much famous Kansas City barbecue and thick steaks, and it's sapping their energy. Their colons are stuffed with undigested meat fibers, almost as bad as Sake's diet of plastic. Now they're as sluggish and sloe-eyed as the cattle they've consumed—at least that's what I tell myself as I wrap up my third set, which ends with scattered applause and almost no tips. The manager tells me the bar did well, that the crowds pick up closer to the weekend. But there are no diamonds within reach tonight.

I finish the gig feeling as if I've made something more difficult than music—that I mined iron ore or milled trees into lumber. My shoulders are stiff and my hands sore. The circuit has become harder lately. In the dressing room mirror, I see an older version of myself, one with more crosshatched lines around the edges of his eyes than before. I tell myself that I've been on the road for weeks, that I just need to sleep late in the morning. But I know the truth, the message we all hide from in one way or another—I'm getting older.

At some point, my looks will fade and my place on the circuit will lower. Places like Riley's don't want to see a geezer at the keys. I'll settle into one hotel lounge or another, playing *Moondance* until I keel over and the bartenders cart me off. I shiver at the thought, not the first glimpse of loneliness and mortality to cross my mind lately.

I retrieve my jacket from the dressing room closet and see a poster of Marianne London smiling at me again. She plays Riley's next week, following me like a sultry shadow. Malcolm tells me she's one of the top draws on his circuit.

The next morning, I sit in the breakfast nook of my room at the Hotel Phillips and read the *Star*. In the Metro section, I read about Food for Free, a local food pantry running low on funds. The article goes on about how many people rely on it, about the single mothers and families. Their shortfall this year isn't that big, just

$5,000, which the director blames on the uncertain economy and a particularly hard winter.

I open the black panel in the back of the fakebook and take out the envelope of cash that was once a silver BMW, now on an extended road trip to Peking. I put the cash in my jacket pocket and take the elevator down to the lobby.

At the downtown post office, I buy four $500 money orders made out to Food for Free, paying cash and signing Charles Parker—clerks never check the name. If you convert more than $2,000, they have to ask to see identification. So then I take a long walk downtown, stopping at a bank and a convenience store to go through the same ritual.

By noon, I have money orders for $5,000. I walk east on 12th Street until I cross Paseo Boulevard, where there's a side street called Ella Fitzgerald Lane. Kansas City honors its musicians. That there will never be a Ross Clifton Lane doesn't bother me. I've given up on normal ambitions.

Other men walking along the sidewalk carry burdens that I can only imagine. They're shuffling from the pressure. They want something—another job, a better life, a bigger house. They're working for the big payoff, gathering money and spending it just like Chief did, just like I used to in the days of Alta, Sake, and the Bösendorfer. But today I drift from the sidewalk up into the eggshell blue prairie sky. I want nothing.

The euphoria passes as it always does, crowded out. I stop across the street from Food for Free's ratty office in a row of brick storefronts. There's a steady flow of people through the front door. A battered white truck pulls up, and volunteers load it up with cartons of cans, flats of day-old bread. No legendary barbecue here. After a few minutes, the truck leaves and the street quiets.

I walk down the sidewalk and shove the envelope into a letter slot, then rush away. In what seems like two seconds, the door bursts open.

"Hey! Come back here!" The voice sounds angry, as if I've just dropped off a letter full of suspicious white powder.

I turn for a moment and see a small group of young volunteers at the office door, squinting into the bright sun at me, the odd visitor who has just left them $5,000.

I turn and run as fast as I can. They bolt after me. Maybe they think the money is stolen or that there's some catch. Or maybe they'd rather chase someone than load trucks.

A young girl in a black T-shirt, red shorts, and white sneakers gains on me.

"Hey, catch him!" she shouts. Others along the sidewalk turn to stare, wondering why this girl is chasing a waiter.

I have no time to savor the irony that I'm being chased for giving away money. All I can do is run. My years of anonymity are about to end. Attention breeds questions, the kind I'd rather not answer, now or ever.

Luckily, I slept late this morning, did my Tibetan exercises, ate miso soup for breakfast, took my vitamins. I finally outdistance the volunteer, dodging along the downtown grid until I can stop running. I kneel forward, hands on my knees, and catch my breath in front of Division Twelve, a nice restaurant in a restored firehouse.

Inside, people read menus, smile at waitresses, settle into pale pink banquettes. Near the back, I see a woman who looks a lot like Marianne London crowded in among a handful of older men, a shimmering jewel in a setting of suits. They raise flutes of champagne high and I hear the glassy clink even out on the street.

"Hey!" The fleet-footed girl—a smeared vision in red, white, and black—speeds toward me.

I start to run again, faster and farther this time.

One summer weekend, Chief loaded us into the Cougar and took us on a road trip to revisit our Wolfshead roots. I was fifteen, sneaking out to clubs at night. Ray was seventeen, running a complicated, lucrative trade selling flashy "rare" coins to trusting fools via the mail. Our mother spent most of her time drinking Sanka with a clutch of angry friends, all in the midst of messy divorces. Chief would be next, she threatened.

Driving toward Coffeyville, Chief dusted off a few chestnuts about his own miserable childhood growing up in Kansas during the Great Depression. He told us about how my grandfather, Big Chief, got his name by spending so much time in the watermelon fields that he turned dark and creased as a Cherokee chief. The origins of my father's name were equally obvious—Chief was always in charge, at home, at work, in the car, everywhere.

Chief told another story about Big Chief and a hired man digging out the chicken house. They scraped down to the hard red clay and then some. The hired man shouted and pulled a rusted tin can from the ground. Inside, they found almost fifteen dollars in change. A fortune.

"He took that money . . ." Chief recalled, voice tightening with rare emotion, "and he gave it all to the hired man. He had every right to keep it—it was on his land, you understand. And he had three kids and the hired man didn't have any. Said it was right for the finder to keep it."

Chief shook his head at his father's foolish generosity. But

I cast our grandfather as the anti-hero of this Dust Bowl tale. It's easy to be generous when you have much; harder when you have nothing; harder still when you have nothing and a family to feed.

"Do you think there were any old ones in there?" Ray asked. "Any gold coins or anything?"

Without taking his eyes from the road, Chief reached his arm over the Cougar's front seat and backhanded Ray's fleshy cheek with a solid slap. Eileen grabbed Chief's arm, asked him to stop.

On the outskirts of Coffeyville we drove down a dusty road lined with towering oil derricks, pumping units, and bright silver tanks. Roughnecks with faces the color of tobacco turned to watch our expensive car raise the dust.

"That's one of the richest, shallowest fields they ever found in the state of Kansas," Chief said, pointing out at the oil-slick land. "You can strike oil with a shovel. And it's still producing all these years later." Again, he shook his head. Big Chief had sold his mineral rights to "an operator from Dallas" shortly before the first well came in—a gusher for someone else.

There was a brief lull in the blackened fields, a green patch of ten acres or so divided by a brown snaky creek. Next to the creek stood a tidy white house with a front porch. On that porch sat my grandfather. I had never met him before this day; when Chief left a place, he left it for good.

"That's him," Chief said. "Go tell him who you are. You got an hour. And I expect in that time you'll get some kind of appreciation for what I'm providing you two . . . just look around this godforsaken place . . ." Chief kicked us out and sat arguing with Eileen in the Cougar. Ray and I stood around on the grass for a few minutes, the heat gathering in my jeans and slicking my legs with sweat.

Big Chief rose as we walked closer, squinting at us and the nice car. "No melons today, boys," he croaked. "Nothing ripe."

Chief had already told us how his father had swallowed gasoline accidentally while siphoning it from a jerrycan into his tractor, how he lay on the ground, paralyzed and paper-white until a field hand hit him in the chest with an axe handle to restart his lungs. His vocal cords were all but burned away, leaving him with only a low croak. He had to swallow air before he spoke, so he said as little as possible.

"I'm Ray Wolfshead, your grandson," Ray shouted, pointing at himself, then at me. "And this is Ross."

"He's not deaf," I whispered. Ray just shrugged.

Big Chief swallowed, croaked. "Should've told me so." A pause. "Got melons for kin."

He led us along a narrow trail past the house and into the greenest patch of land I had ever seen. A small garden held rows of tomatoes growing up a trapeze of twine. Runner beans climbed an old paint-splattered wooden ladder left in the garden to rot. Dark rows of collards stretched toward the river.

Then we came to the watermelon vines, growing thick as garden hoses from mounds of reddish earth, trailing off into fuzzy leaves, yellow blossoms, and the glimmer of dark green-striped skins.

"Black Beauty," he said pointing at one row. "Redwing," he said of another. "Flesh is red." A wheezing pause. "Sugarbowl. Super-sweet."

He waded carefully into the vines, then stopped for a moment and reached down to grab something from the ground—a whip, it seemed—and snapped it hard once, then tossed it toward us, laughing. Ray and I stared at the rattlesnake, three feet long, pink mouth glistening.

"Ever seen . . . one of them?" he croaked, already too far into the watermelon patch to hear our answer. We hadn't, and never would again.

Ray and I stood silently next to the still-writhing snake, my clothes suddenly too crisp and new, face too pale, hands too soft. We had stumbled into a primeval land. The fields around us seemed dangerously alive, as if the vines coursed up from the heart of the world. My safe life and Ray's devious plans paled and shriveled in comparison.

Our grandfather came back with a green-black watermelon cradled in his arms. He placed it on the gray boards of an ancient table in the cleared land on the edge of the field. He pulled a curved knife from the wood, quickly traced the blade across the skin.

The melon split in four pieces, orange with seeds big as coat buttons. He handed both of us a quarter and took one himself. He picked up a restaurant saltshaker from the table and waved it over the melon, then smelled it, savoring it before biting away at the flesh.

After a brief pause, Ray and I dove in, standing in the shifting sunlight and holding our melon wedges aloft like an ancient sacrifice. We gorged ourselves on the orange flesh, sunwarm and sweet, juice dripping down our chins and into the dust.

Big Chief smiled at us, city rats, but still his grandsons. I hated Chief suddenly for keeping us away from this benevolent, silent giant for so long, for making us part of his complete erasure of the past. Then Big Chief reached over and sprinkled salt on our melon as well.

"Sweeter this way," he said. "Need the salt to . . ." a deep wheeze, "taste the sweet."

Ray and I bit into the flesh. He was right—the flavor was stronger now, like summer sun in a black-green rind.

When we were done, our grandfather pointed toward a ditch full of rotting rinds and we tossed ours among them. Then he wiggled his thick fingers to draw us forward. Ray leaned over the shallow ditch and Big Chief poured water from a plastic jug over his head to wash the sweet melon juice from his cheeks.

Ray shook his head like a dog and he laughed, then I stepped up, felt the cool water rain down on me.

Chief sounded the horn and I turned toward its insistent honking.

"Time for you to go," Big Chief croaked without sadness. He pointed toward the car.

"We'll come back," Ray said. But we never would. Ray held up his hand, waving goodbye.

Big Chief's brown face wrinkled at the sight of Ray's Casio watch with its complicated settings and tiny buttons. "Don't wear that when you go to sleep," he said.

Ray squinted, confused. Even then, he was a big fan of technology.

"Gives you bad dreams," Big Chief said softly, "sleeping with a wristwatch on." Then he turned and walked back into the melon fields, leaving us to walk in silence to our father, his car, a long trip north.

When my gigs at Riley's are over—three nice diamonds, two BMW conversions—I drive south toward Dallas, past the exit for Coffeyville. There's nothing for me to see there anymore. Big Chief's farm is an oilfield now. Lost in the red dirt there might be a dried length of watermelon vine, the rusted top of a saltshaker. Big Chief is buried just outside of town in a plain plot next to a Coffeyville cowboy yodeler with a gravestone inlaid with cheap rhinestones that spelled out HIS LAST ROUNDUP. Chief took a picture and e-mailed it to me.

I have some gigs out on the West Coast, then I'm in Dallas for a couple of nights, then the road never ends. I have work to do, turning eighty-eight keys into music, notes into melodies, diamonds and BMWs into cash.

dallas

A tall, skinny guy in a gray hooded sweatshirt slumps against the wall next to my hotel room. His hood is pulled down so low that I can't see his face. It's long past midnight. I assume he's asleep or passed out. But maybe he's just pretending. I walk slowly toward him. A long, lucrative evening with an advertising executive netted ten diamonds from a tennis bracelet. I don't want this stranger to steal them; they're mine, for now.

The stranger stirs. He rises and stands swaying in the middle of the hallway.

"UncleRoss?"

I look closer. "Cray?"

"That's right, UncleRoss." He says my name in one slurred package, a brand-name uncle like UncleSam or UncleTom.

I smile thinly. "Ray said you might meet me somewhere."

"Isn't this Providence?"

"It's Dallas."

"I thought people were talking funny," he says. "And wearing boots."

I try not to look disappointed that Cray has managed to hunt me down. But it's hard.

"Ho ho, Uncle Ross, really. I know I'm in Dallas, believe me. If you took the bus all the way from Vermont, you'd know exactly where you were too." He pauses and pulls his hood away, revealing a big tangled mass of straw-colored hair. "Hey, do I smell like citrus-scented bathroom disinfectant?"

He leans his head forward and I smell no hint of citrus, just cigarettes. "No."

"Good."

I open the door and Cray walks in, throwing his backpack on the floor. "Television. Minibar. Bathtub. Heaven," he says softly. He walks to the minibar and cracks off the plastic lock, then takes out an Amstel Light and flips the top off with one deft twist. "Mind if I have a cold one, Uncle Ross?" he says. Before I can answer, he drinks half of the beer. "Traveling makes me wicked thirsty."

I perch on the other bed opposite my nephew. Since I last saw him he's changed from shy to bold, innocent to canny.

"Good to see you, Cray," I say. "Ray told me he needed a little time alone."

Cray rolls his eyes. "Jackson's getting a makeover. Like I'm going to interfere or something. Dad just gets all weird and nervous when he's working. You know how he is, Uncle Ross. Anyway, I'm just glad to get out of freaking Vermont for a while."

"I thought you liked it there."

Cray turns to me and gives me a flat stare that means I have to be kidding. He jumps up and turns the television around. "I'm still a little wired from the bus ride. I drank a couple of those energy drink things," he says. "Mind if I watch something?"

I want to mention that it's late and I've got to be on the road to Little Rock early. Or to be accurate, *we* have to get on the road early tomorrow.

The television flickers on. Cray operates the complicated remote like a pilot.

"How long are you going to be traveling with me?" I ask carefully.

"You mean how long am I going to be bothering you?" Cray scratches his head, smells his fingertips, reaches for his beer.

"Yes, that. But not really."

"A month or so. But I'll stay way out of your way. I'm just along for the ride. I'll be like an invisible passenger. You won't even know I'm here."

I say nothing, just think of the weeks of shows ahead and wonder how I'm going to get any nightwork done with Cray around. He's not the quiet boy he was last summer. He's not a boy at all.

Cray turns to me, reading my thoughts. "You don't have to do anything special, Uncle Ross. Just do what you normally do. Pretend I'm not here." He pulls one grease-stained boot off, then another, and lets them thunk to the floor. Then he pulls the bedspread up to his chin, smiles at a cartoon of a flying dog.

"*Underdog, sweet,*" he whispers. "I fucking love *Underdog.*"

I take off my shoes and hang my suit on a hanger. I pull on a white T-shirt and climb into my bed, the sheets cold against my legs.

"I'm tired," I say.

"Long day tickling the ivories?" I hear overtones of Ray's sneery voice.

"You could say that. I'm going to sleep now."

"Don't let me stop you."

I shut off the lamp on my bedside table. It's dark in the room except for the low blue flame of television. Underdog circles a city.

"Anything new happening with you?" I ask, hoping Cray will turn off the TV.

"Not much. We'll get caught up tomorrow."

"Okay," I say, not at all sure whether that's good news or not.

We've been driving for about thirty minutes when Cray yanks off his headphones and tells me to stop.

I pull into the emergency lane and he jumps out of the car, leaps the guardrail, and scrambles up a gravel slope to a scraggly patch of woods. At checkout, I noticed six Amstel Lights on my bill. From a distance, I can't hear him retching up his breakfast—bacon, eggs, toast, coffee, juice, and hash browns with hot sauce dumped all over them.

I wait for a few minutes in blessed silence. Cray filled the hotel room with his nonstop talking this morning while I was packing. In the end, I just tossed everything into my suitcase and left. I go through my upcoming gigs, tracing the route northeast through Little Rock to Louisville then over to the East Coast for a few weeks, winding up in New York and Boston. The idea of spending all that time with Cray in tow makes me cringe. I'm exhausted after one morning.

I remember that he's only sixteen, that he's my nephew. I just have to come up with a way of being around him. I try to think of Cray as a troubled young man who needs my help, a teenager from a halfway house. Cray actually *was* raised in a barn— growing up with a homeschooling felon for a father and no mother around. Tired of living in lockdown, Linda, Ray's wife, fled to northern California years ago to join an intentional community that raised goats and sold cheese.

I hold this benevolent notion of Cray for a few minutes, then it drifts away and is replaced by less kind thoughts. I look in the rearview mirror and see a ridiculous, fussy man, angry at having his little routine interrupted. What would Miles do?

Cray climbs over the hill carrying a paper bag. Fully recovered, he jumps into the car.

"Sorry you were feeling sick." I pull back onto the highway.

"Sick? Not me. Just hungry." Cray holds up a football-sized foil package. "Hombre Grande," he says. "Saw the sign from the highway. Hombre Grande Special. Doesn't that mean Big Man in Spanish?"

"Yes, it does."

"Dad's going to love this one." Cray unrolls the foil package and reveals a burrito the size of a toddler. He pokes it with a fork and eats a bite, dropping bits of rice and brown meat onto the floor. The car fills with the smell of pig fat and refried beans. I open my window a crack.

"Dad collects burritos," Cray says between bites, or during them.

"Probably hard to fit in an album."

"Not the actual food, Uncle Ross, *duh*. We just write up its name and a description of what's in it in a little book we keep in the kitchen. *Burrito Grande. Bueno Burrito. Salsa Burrito. Burrito de Casa.* It's amazing how many words there are for the same damn thing. Like Eskimos have all those words for snow. Mexicans got them for burritos." Cray lifts the Mexican child and takes a bite out of its soft white middle.

I put on my sunglasses and turn back to the road. "So you like Mexican food?" I say after a minute.

"No, not really." Cray shakes his head. "It's just that you can't get it in Vermont. They're always rolling up alfalfa sprouts and carrots in a whole-wheat wrap and calling it a burrito. That is NOT A BURRITO," he shouts. It is the most vehement statement he has made so far, second only to his opinion that hotels are a BIG DAMN RIP-OFF, which he offered at checkout this morning.

"Now Uncle Ross, I know you're a vegan," Cray says with complete disdain. "But you got to remember, I'm from health food ground zero. I can get a wheatgrass shot pretty much every hundred yards in Montpelier. And the place is thick with organic cafés that serve . . ." He puts down the Mexican child and shakes his head slowly.

"You okay?"

His voice turns serious. "It's just that . . . can I share something, Uncle Ross? Something kind of personal?"

"Sure, Cray."

"This winter I met this girl who worked at a place called the Common Street Bakery, right in the center of town. They serve smoothies and salads and all that shit you like. Anyway, this girl Angelina used to cook there. She wore these short, tight T-shirts that showed off her incredible body. She had hooters that—"

I hold up my hand. "Spare me the details, please, Cray."

"Oh, yeah. Dad mentioned you were a little weird about, well, you know," Cray says.

I stare, wonder what Ray told him.

"And when she turned around, I could see she had these tattoos on her back, those *f*-shaped things, you know what I mean?"

"Like on a violin?"

"Exactly. Well for some reason, she had them tattooed on her back. And believe me, Uncle Ross, I wanted to play that violin."

"I believe you."

Cray leans forward and places his Mexican child, swaddled in foil, on the seat. "Anyway, I sat at the counter for hours just to watch her. I drank banana smoothies. I had salads with zen sauce on them—I'm not even sure what the hell zen sauce is. But I would have eaten bugs just to sit there and watch her."

"Did you talk to her?"

Cray says nothing, turns away. "All winter. These long intense talks. Then one day, she said she could never love anyone who . . . wore leather shoes. Uncle Ross, does that seem fair to you? She said you should never eat or wear anything that once had a face." Cray turns his own reddening face away, holds his palm toward me.

"Well, I have to say, I kind of agree with her on that one."

"But isn't that a bit . . . judgmental? I mean, can people only be with people who are just like them? What about diversity? What about opposites attracting? How do you explain that?" Cray turns to the window. "I think she could have been my only true love, Uncle Ross, and I lost her on account of MY DIET and MY FOOTWEAR. It just makes me really, really sad." Cray's narrow shoulders rise and fall.

I try to come up with something consoling. "I'm sure you'll meet someone else. You're too young to worry about that."

"That's easy for you to say," he whispers. "You're old."

We travel in silence, Cray watching the low trees and grassy hills unwind before us.

"I'm really sorry," I say.

"About what?"

"About that girl you were talking about. The one from the restaurant."

Cray's shoulders start to rise and fall again.

"I'm sure you'll meet someone else, Cray." I glance over and see that Cray isn't crying anymore. He's laughing.

"Uncle Ross, I totally made that up. You're still as gullible as the day is long." Cray picks up his burrito and takes a vigorous bite that reminds me of a wasp stinging a peach.

I roll down my window carefully, then reach over with one hand, grab *Hombre Grande* from Cray, and toss it out. In the rearview mirror, I watch the big man bounce along in the underbrush for a few moments before deconstructing into a brown cloud.

"Hey, I wasn't done with that!"

"You are now, *hombre*."

We drive silently again, northeast Texas racing by in a smear of stunted trees and rolling hills dotted with black cattle. Cray puts his headphones back on, silver and sleek with a wire that runs down into a bulging pocket of his orange cargo pants. He nods his head.

I watch the yellow lines ticking past, each one taking us

closer to Arkansas. I never like playing there—low on BMWs and good diamonds. But I've never been so anxious to see Little Rock, where I can put more than two feet between me and my passenger, his eyes shut tightly, oblivious to me, the world.

Cray sleeps, headphones on, head pressed against the passenger window. The afternoon shifts into a minor key, amber sunlight turning even the most egregious roadside rest stops and gas stations into Hopper landscapes. I think of waking Cray to show him, but why bother?

As soon as that thought passes through my mind, I realize that too much time alone has left me hyper-attuned to landscapes, less so to the people in them. But then again, driving draws out budget insights.

We drive across a flat stretch of highway, the billboards old and advertising motels that no longer exist, bungalows for thirty dollars. Cray turns in his sleep, avoiding the bright sun. I peer through my sunglasses at the road ahead, see it waver in the heat.

Cray is one of the last relatives I have left, but I can't seem to muster up much empathy for him, even though I know he needs it. He's lost, just the same way I was at his age. Why can't I help him more? After all, I've given stacks of money to complete strangers, but I'm almost incapable of being in the same car with Cray. I wonder if I've become too solitary after years on the road or if I'm allergic to my family.

The Wolfshead family is receding day after day until there is nothing left except the loaded memories Ray and I carry with us, filtered even further by Cray, the latest generation of the deft and devious.

But I don't particularly want to explore our mutual history or the connections that make us relatives instead of strangers. I just want to stop, shove Cray out by the side of the road, and drive away.

"I'm going to write a novel," Cray announces out of the blue, lifting his headphones and leaving them around his neck.

I slow, take the exit to Little Rock. "I didn't know you had literary ambitions."

Cray makes a scrunched face. "I don't. I just want to make a big pile of money."

"Why don't you just have Dad print some?"

"I mean real money, Uncle Ross, and a segment on *E!* or some shit like that." Cray nods, his eyes widen a bit. "That would be way cool. The chicks at the organic place would be all over me like nori flakes on brown rice."

"So what would it be about?"

"The thing on *E!*? It would be all about me, dumbass."

"I mean the book. The book you'd write to get an article written about you."

"It would be about . . ." Cray pauses, searching. "It would be about love."

"About love, that sounds interesting."

"Ho ho, Uncle Ross, I don't think you know what I mean. You're thinking some kind of nice novel where two people meet and find they're soulmates and wind up walking through poppy fields and holding hands. Isn't that what you're thinking about?"

"Not exactly, but close enough."

"I'm talking about a book that gets rid of all that crap and just gets right down to it, Uncle Ross. Two people doing it every ten pages or so, without any worrying about all the long conversations, details that no one cares about, fancy descriptions no one really reads. Just following the natural buildup and release of sexual tension. We're talking genitals, Uncle Ross. Genitals and friction."

"Aren't those the two motivating forces in Greek drama?"

"Uh, I'm not sure. Maybe."

"I think you're on to something, Cray."

"I know I am, Uncle Ross. I know what people like. And it isn't being bored by some smarty-pants author trying to impress them with all the crap he knows."

The car goes silent.

"I need a great title." He concentrates for a minute, squinting and working his mouth into various shapes. "I think I might call it *The Good Parts,*" he says finally.

"Won't that kind of take the mystery out of the whole thing, Cray?"

"Uncle Ross, people DO NOT WANT MYSTERY. THEY DO NOT WANT SUBTLETY. They want lusty full-frontal action. That's why they invented the Internet—to bring porn to the people, pronto. Books are lagging way behind. That's why no one buys them anymore."

"But you'll take care of that."

"Yes I will, Uncle Ross. Yes I will. I'll just do a little of this on my computer." Cray holds both hands horizontally in front of him and hammers his fingers up and down. "Soon as I get home."

"Can't wait to read it, Cray."

"You'll get the first copy, signed, Uncle Ross. Seeing you in action out here on the road has really inspired me."

I look over at Cray slouching in the passenger seat. "To write a porn novel?"

"No, to do what I want to do. And not worry what other people say about it."

"Well, that part sounds fine, Cray. I'll just tell you what I tell people who want to play music—don't quit your day job."

"I don't even have a day job, Uncle Ross."

"Exactly."

little rock

Midway through my second set at the Embassy Club, a familiar figure glides into the bar and takes a seat at a table in the back. He wears a gray fedora, aviator shades, a dark suit, and a white shirt. He gives me a small nod, acknowledging that he's here to really listen, that he's a musician, that he knows me. The connection isn't clear.

I start into *My Romance,* slow it down to match the crowd, full of introspective couples staring into their drinks. I'm having trouble getting over and the audience isn't doing its part to fulfill the unwritten entertainer-audience contract.

I've already tried the usual tricks—playing a fast series, songs everyone knows, a couple of flashy solos. Nothing I play gets much of a response. The audience is involved in a collective and detailed study of the ice cubes in their drink glasses. I go through the set one song after the next, my hands moving along the keys without much thought.

I'm wondering about Cray. The last hundred miles of our drive passed in a blur of conversation, or more accurately, a *non-versation,* since Cray did all the talking. I try to listen. But since he told me about his fake girlfriend, all of Cray's stories sound like lies, the kind that would wither under casual scrutiny. He hacked the Web site for the state of Vermont and changed the governor's name to Smoksa B. Igdube. He aced his SATs without studying. He plays an online game called DragonSlayer so well that he has a cult following in Japan. He exposed a local minister as a *freaking pornaholic* and got him run out of town. Typed, printed, and bound, the lies he's told me would fill a small bookshelf.

I wish I could be a good uncle to Cray, that I could care about all his problems. But I just want to be free of him. I've been alone for too long to be flexible. My routine is deep and unshakable. I want only to play the piano, steal, and give away the money. Is that asking too much?

Instead, Cray is relentlessly with me—talking, turning on the radio, television, anything that makes noise. I realize that this is what it's like to be old, capable only of saying *no* in various ways.

I look at my hands. I'm somewhere in the middle of *How High the Moon,* though I don't remember starting the song. I think of Les Paul, dead now, who must have played this song thousands of times on his guitar, Mary Ford perched next to him. When he had the car wreck that shattered his right arm, Les Paul told his doctors to set his arm bent at an angle so he could strum the strings of his guitar. After that, he could be a guitarist, nothing else. Had I become just as inflexible? If my rental car wandered off into a guardrail and flipped into the woods by the side of the interstate, would I have my mangled arms set at forty-five-degree angles so I could always rest my hands on the keyboard?

No one in the entire bar except the familiar stranger in the back seems to be paying attention. He orders another drink with a confident wiggle of his fingers. Then he points his index finger at me and clicks an imaginary pistol, tilting his head back with a soundless laugh. I squint, unable to figure out who he is. My fans tend to be oddballs who spend way too much time at home listening to scratchy records.

During my last song, *Our Love Is Here to Stay,* I recognize the black jacket the stranger wears. It's my backup jacket, a lesser Armani hidden in my suit bag. The shirt is white with a spread collar, my favorite. I look closer, realize that the stranger looks more than familiar. He looks like family. He raises his glass in a sloppy toast. His eyes are inscrutable behind his aviator shades, face shaded by the fedora. But his shiny head-phones glimmer in the light from the candle flickering on his table.

I botch a bass chord, then recover. It was incredibly naïve to leave Cray watching television in our room. I bring the song back together, add a little four-bar solo to end it, then thump down five or six strong final chords to rush the ending and finish off the set.

The clinically depressed people who've made up my audience

for the last two hours make polite, perfunctory applause, like grade-schoolers after a boring assembly. I won't be coming back for an encore. Now they are free to head back to their Little Rock ranch houses and watch televangelists or porn, eat microwave popcorn, e-mail secret friends, review their stock portfolios— whatever people here do at one A.M. on a Friday night.

I stay in the back room for a moment, washing my hands and pouring a glass of soda water. The club owner isn't around, just the bar staff, only slightly more animated than its patrons. Now that I'm done, they blast the sound system. I peer out at the crowd nodding along to Booker T. and the M.G.'s and smiling at the welcome sound of Motown. The musicians who recorded this song decades ago in Detroit could never have guessed that they would make so many white people so happy for so long.

Cray is still sitting at his table, but he has some new friends now, two couples who have dragged over their chairs to huddle with him. He raises his hand in the air, pale wrist poking out of my too-small suit. He points a crisp bill toward the ceiling, summoning the waitress and more drinks. The new friends laugh at something Cray says. Annoyed as I am at my nephew, I'm also impressed at his brazen ways, so different from the low profile I kept when I was sneaking into clubs.

I wander over to the bar manager, a blond woman, thirty or so, who wears two diamond studs in each ear. We talk for a moment, pleasantries that fill the time while she looks for my check in the cash register drawer. If I spent a few hours with her, she might tell me how she ended up spraying ginger ale from a little hose into glasses, pushing tips into the pocket of a shiny black apron. But she's ringless and her earrings are crap. I take my check, thank her, then walk through the thinning club to Cray's table.

"Hey, it's my . . . brother," Cray says in a voice that sounds remarkably like Ray's.

I nod.

"Nice set." He points to an empty seat. "Chill with us for a few minutes."

I shake my head, turn to the others at the table, smile. "If you wouldn't mind, we have some family business to discuss."

They pick up their drinks and move slowly to another table, disappointed that the fun is over.

"Really nice to meet you all," Cray calls after them, smiling. "Enjoy your conference."

I push my face close to his and smell beer. "What are you do-ing?"

"Having a drink or three with some new friends," he says. "What're you doing?"

"I'm working. And wondering how long I can put up with this," I say. "That's what I'm doing."

"Put up with what?" Cray lowers his sunglasses.

"With stunts like this." I point to his clothes, the empty beer glass in front of him.

"Okay, so I ordered some drinks," Cray says. "No big deal. I paid for them myself. And I'll pay to have your suit pressed. Here." He picks up a pile of bills from the table and waves them at me.

I hold up my palm. "I don't want your money."

"What then?"

"I need you to not cause any trouble," I say, instantly hating how I sound, so much like Chief scolding Ray and me as boys.

Cray leans forward, drains his glass. "I think you need a little more trouble, Uncle Ross. If this is the way you're spending your time . . ." He glances around the club, nearly empty now. "Then you definitely need to change something."

"Maybe."

"What are relatives for, then?" Cray says. "I'm here to help you out, Uncle Ross, you'll see. Just like the *Cat in the Hat*, remember what he said?"

"No."

"*I'm here to help you have some fun.*"

"Thanks for that." We get up to leave.

"I'm full of exceptionally wide-ranging knowledge," Cray says, then stumbles.

I catch his arm and lead him toward the door. "Full of beer, too."

"Yes, beer and knowledge," he says. "What could be a better combination?"

"I suppose a burrito might add something," I say.

Cray brightens, turns to point at me. "Now you're thinking, Uncle Ross. Now you're really thinking."

Out on the highway, Cray slumps against the window. He's asleep, I think, blind to the lush farmland rolling by. We spent a couple of hours in the hotel room last night, talking about how to get along during the weeks ahead. Cray agreed to stay out of trouble and I agreed to let him drink two Amstel Lights every night in the hotel room. He promised not to lie to me and I promised not to bother him about his diet. We shook on it and went to sleep in a détente that seems to be holding in the light of morning.

Cray stirs, then reaches into his backpack and takes out a thick stack of twenties. He snaps off the rubber band and pulls off the first bill, crumples it into a ball, then straightens it with a practiced twist. He presses the button to roll down the window slightly, then feeds the bill through the gap, turns to watch it float off into the weeds by the roadside.

I say nothing.

Ten minutes later Cray is still jettisoning bills one after the other.

"What're you doing?" I try to sound uninterested.

Cray startles, pulls off his headphones. "What, Uncle Ross?"

"I was just wondering what you were doing, Cray."

He holds up the stack of bills. "Helping Dad. He asked me to put these into circulation." Cray peels off another bill, crumples it, straightens it, and sets it free on the highway.

"Counterfeit, I assume."

Cray shakes his head. "Dad isn't a counterfeiter, Uncle Ross. He's way beyond that. He's a *currency anticipator.*"

"What does that mean?"

Cray holds up a twenty. "Okay, see the back here, where it shows the White House with all those weird little yellow numbers raining down on it? They're changing the tree on the left in a month or so. They're adding a hidden pattern, microprinting it's called, to keep the regular counterfeiters guessing. Dad's already on top of it." He held the twenty near the window and let the wind suck it outside. "*Counterfeiting is for amateurs, anticipating is art.* That's what he says."

"How does he know what they're going to change?"

Cray rolls his eyes. "Because that's all he thinks about. He's beyond obsessed, Uncle Ross. He even pays some guy in Washington to steal trash from the Committee of Four. You probably don't even know who they are, do you?"

"No, Cray. I don't. Sounds kind of ominous and Chinese."

"It's a committee at the Bureau of Engraving that figures out what changes to make to our dollar bills. Top secret stuff. It's headed by James D. Croton."

"Who?"

"Some government dweeb who runs the whole currency division. I think Dad's just jealous, if you ask me. He's always talking about Croton, trying to make him look bad. You remember back when they switched over to the big-headed portrait on the twenty, *the ugly money,* Dad calls it?"

"Yes." I remember an endless stream of twenties shoved in mailboxes, mailed in envelopes, slipped beneath doors.

"Dad was on top of that. FedExed a Jackson to Croton in Washington on the day they announced the changes. That's what being a currency anticipator is all about. Now he's so far into the future that it's spooky. He knows what the twenty-dollar bill is going to look like three years from now."

"I bet. So, Cray, what do you think about his career?"

"I'm proud of him," Cray says. "He works hard. He's devoted to what he does. And he's not just trying to make a lot of money like most of the other dads I know."

"He's just trying to print a lot of money."

"That's just it, Uncle Ross. He could print a lot of money, but he doesn't. Just enough."

"Enough to what?"

"Survive. *To introduce doubt into the system,* is what he says. *Doubt, not debt.* And stay under the radar."

"So no one knows what he does?"

Cray shakes his head. "Everyone thinks Dad's a printer. A really good one."

"What if they ask what he prints?"

"I tell them he prints art books. The expensive kind. And in a way, what he does really is art, Uncle Ross. I mean, check this out." He holds up a twenty-dollar bill and I take it in one hand.

I look away from the road for a moment. "Looks real to me."

"That's because it is," Cray said. "I was just testing you." He peels off another twenty-dollar bill. "Here's one of Dad's."

"That looks pretty good too," I say. "Maybe not quite as crisp."

"That's actually a real one, too, Uncle Ross. I was testing you again." He hands me another twenty. "Here, this is hot off the Heidelberg."

"Now I don't know whether to believe you," I say. "It could be real or not."

"Bingo!" Cray shouts. "That's exactly it. People *should* wonder whether it's real or not. It's just a piece of fancy paper and some ink. It's not really worth anything. Dad says that when the country went off the gold standard it was the beginning of the end. Everything's bogus now. That's why the markets keep freaking out."

"I might have to agree with him on that one. Except gold isn't really worth anything either. There's just less of it than paper."

Cray reaches up and stretches his arms, presses his hands up on the ceiling of the car, leaving greasy smears. "I'll tell you one thing, Uncle Ross."

"What's that?"

"You think about money differently when you see stacks of it lined up in your barn."

"I bet."

"I see people getting all weird about money and I think, what's the fuss? It's just a symbol someone told us we had to respect, like the flag. Or Jesus. Or Hallmark cards. When someone sends you some stupid card, you're supposed to think it means they care. The Hallmark people made us think this through advertising or whatever, and their brand gets a monopoly on caring. And most people believe it. But if you don't, then when you get a Hallmark card you're like—HEY, WHAT A STUPID-ASS THING TO SEND ME. GO FUCK YOURSELF. WHY DIDN'T YOU JUST WRITE ME A LETTER OR, BETTER YET, TALK TO ME?" Cray stops shouting, rubs his face, settles. "It's like that with money, too, in a way."

Cray seems to take in all the world's input—my brother's rants, blogs, television, ads—and reflect it back out into the world like a chrome-plated oracle. I hear Ray's angry voice intertwined with Cray's uncertainty. *Ray and Cray*—what was my brother thinking? The father carried within the son.

We pass a sign—110 miles to go. It's going to be a long afternoon.

"I mean, you're scrambling around the country, getting paid to play the piano in front of a bunch of drunk chicks and sad sacks and geezers. Doesn't it just seem kind of stupid to you sometimes?"

"Of course it does." I'm tempted to tell Cray about my secret life, to point out that I do more than simply wiggle my fingers. But I stop short of any road trip revelations. Despite our current détente, I'm not sure that I trust Cray to keep a secret. To keep anything.

"Then why do you do it? For money?"

"I like to play the piano. And sometimes you have to put up with a certain amount of shit to do something that you really like to do."

"You know what I should do with my life, Uncle Ross?"

"No."

He shrugs. "Neither do I, really. I mean, I just don't want to end up like you or Dad, doing the same thing over and over. With minor variations, know what I mean?"

I press my eyes closed and swerve into the emergency lane for a moment, then open my eyes and pull back into my lane.

"Here's what I like to do." Cray counts off his favorite things on his fingers. "I like talking to girls. I like to drink beer. I like rock climbing and skiing. I like playing DragonSlayer. I like walking around town without having any idea of where I'll end up. That pretty much sums it up."

"You'll figure out something that you want to do."

"Everyone says that."

"But I mean it. I wouldn't send you a Hallmark card, Cray."

"I know you wouldn't," he says, then pulls on his headphones, done with me for a while, turning to other voices to guide him as we drive across a long bridge, the coffee-colored Mississippi roiling below.

I met the man who pointed me toward my future one night when he was playing in Chicago at a dive bar called the Top Spot. Delmar Robbins might be my mentor, but that sounds too much like he was training me to be a jazz executive. The French word *passeur* is closer to his role—someone who brought me into a new world, a ferryman into nightlife.

Delmar played fewer notes than anyone I had ever seen play the piano. Watching from a rickety front table, I could see that he was putting his hands, flat-fingered as Monk's, where they needed to be to play the entire melody, but just tracing it out with a spare fill or two, stabbing the keys. He turned a standard like *Embraceable You* into an unrecognizable minimalist work-out. Sometimes I couldn't even remember what song he was playing—they were only a place to start.

Like Cray, I was sixteen, fast-talking, wise-ass, naïve. But I knew that I'd found someone who could point the way.

Delmar was a sonic housewrecker; he brought down the walls of a song with sledgehammer chords to let sunlight in. He seemed furious at the keyboard, swinging at some leftover scrap of melody hanging stubbornly at the end of a run. Delmar was a painter, sketching only the outline of what he wanted the audience to see, sometimes just a couple of points, leaving us to draw the lines.

I failed to notice the truth—Delmar Robbins was one of the laziest piano players in the world. He was simply trying to play as few notes as possible because it elevated the amount he was being paid *per note,* notes being the commodity that he brought to the club.

I was mesmerized night after night, following Delmar up and down the row of almost-bankrupt, legendary clubs where I was always the youngest and straightest in the audience. Others were drinking, talking, trying to forget about work or find a new lover. I was there to watch Delmar's hands. When he caught me, he would slip his right hand into his jacket pocket and play the rest of the song with just his left—an old Phineas Newborn trick, though I didn't know it then—and wink at me.

On a Saturday night when Chief and Eileen thought I was stay-ing over at a friend's house, I talked my way into Tim's Cast-away Club, a club packed with secretaries and their bosses, hipster couples, drug addicts, and drunks—in short, perennial nightclubbers.

Delmar's bleary face hovered inches over the keyboard, right hand tracing a melodic outline, left hand smacking its way through the bass like a blind man. He shot me a look, one that told me to pay attention. He sat bolt upright for a moment, hands in the air. Then he attacked the keys, lowering his head slowly as he played four bars of breakneck melody. His forehead hovered over the keys, fingers racing, eyes closing in rapture. In all, the downward plunge took about ten seconds. Then he played the same complicated four bars backward while backing his forehead away from the keys and rearing up suddenly. His eyes popped open and his fingers jerked away from the keys as if they had suddenly heated up like a sidewalk in August.

The crowd jumped to its feet, applauding. Glasses shattered on the floor. I stood on my chair and watched as Delmar played the same four bars backward and forward, over and over. I don't remember the song; it's unimportant. The effect, though, is etched into my memory. Delmar stopped time, reversed it, then started it up again. Delmar was tinkering with the order of the universe, reversing the world's inevitable spin.

I had never seen or heard anything like it. I already knew that every player had tricks to help get over with an audience. But this was more than a trick.

That night I walked up to Delmar after his set was over and the crowd had thinned out. I opened my mouth and an embarrassing paragraph of praise and ambition and youth popped out like a shiny lozenge. To this day, I cringe when I remember it, even though Delmar is long dead.

A pause. A long pause. Four beats at least, then Delmar spoke. "You got twenty green dollars, boy?"

I did. I took out my wallet and gave the money to him.

He smiled, revealed a dentist's nightmare of twisted teeth and blackened gums. "Looking good. Now I can show you some things. Set right down here." He patted the bench next to him.

I'd like to be able to say that over the next few months, Delmar taught me the inner secrets of the legendary jazzman, that he saw me as his pale protégé. A hundred dollars later, he did teach me how to do the trick that turned back time. But most of his teachings were more practical.

Never play out on Monday night.

Use a clear tip jar and seed it with a five, not anything larger. (Who're you kidding?)

Audition a sideman by making him play something he's never heard before.

Order a set from the middle, putting your best songs there.

When the club is dead, play slow songs for a while, then a jump number.

Get paid up front and in cash.

Don't play for a cut of the door.

Never rush the ending.

This was the wisdom of Delmar Robbins, someone never mentioned in any jazz book or found on any dusty record. It's as if he never existed. But to me, he was as real and unknowable as Miles.

memphis

Ray calls late at night, as always.

"How's life with my boy?"

I click on the light. "Fine. If you like hearing someone talking all the time." I look across the room at Cray, silent only because he's asleep.

Ray laughs. "Yeah, he's kind of a one-man orchestra, except he doesn't know how to play an instrument. A virtuoso chatterbox. Driving you nuts yet?"

I say nothing.

"I'll take that as a *yes*."

"More like maybe."

"Just tell him to shut up if he's bugging you. He'll pipe down. He's a smart guy—aced his SATs, without even studying."

I stop for a moment. "He told me that, but I didn't believe him."

"He tell you anything else you want to check out?"

"Did he hack the state Web site?"

"Smoksa B. Igdube." Ray laughs. "Got to like that one."

"What about DragonSlayer?"

"That totally violent game he plays all the time? He's a whiz at anything involving computers. Gets about a dozen e-mails a week from Japanese fans, wondering why he hasn't been playing lately. All of Tokyo mourns his departure."

"What about the minister, the one he . . ."

"Got booted out of town? Reverend Phil the porno priest? Kid's got a righteous streak in him a mile wide. Hates it when someone takes advantage of someone else."

I wonder how Cray might feel about my nightwork.

"I'll give you a little bit of advice that will help you decode Cray," Ray says. "When he decides to lie, he's good. Masterful, even. You believe every word of it. Ought to run for office. Or be an actor. The fuckin' kid can cry on command, for crissakes."

"Impressive."

"But when he's telling the truth, it sounds like a big damn lie."

"I just thought he liked to make things up."

"Not really. He's kind of ruthless about honesty."

"He's kind of ruthless about everything."

"If he gets too intense, just give him an Amstel Light. Don't let him drink those energy drink things. They make him weird."

"No kidding."

"*One weak, one weird,*" Ray says. "Remember that one?"

My smile fades. "Yes." This was the way Chief used to refer to us, as in, *these are my sons, one weak and one weird.*

"Never did tell us which was which, did he?"

"No."

"I'd ask him, but we're kind of out of touch."

"I haven't talked to him in months." Retired now, Chief's life in Washington involves a lot of high-profile charity events, photos in the *Post,* and consulting assignments for the Department of Labor.

"Oh yeah, one other thing about Cray, he's not like us."

"What do you mean?"

"Remember all the stunts we pulled as kids—stealing things, scams, all our little operations?"

"Sure."

"Well, we pretty much got away with them, right?"

"Yeah, most of them."

"Cray can't get away with anything. Gets busted time and again. He's destined for the straight and narrow."

I shake my head. "Shame."

"Maybe it's better, ever thought of that?"

"No, not really."

"Me neither. Never an option." The phone clicks and Ray's gone.

A woman in a white jacket sits near the front of the club during my set. She has blond hair and wears a flashy platinum ring on her right hand, the hand that the diamond people have dubbed the "me" hand, as opposed to the "we" hand that signifies marriage. Her ring catches the light every few minutes and sends a spectrum arcing through the room. Though I try to ignore her, she captures my every glance, as does her ring.

At the end of my last set, I find myself drawn to her, though I know I should just go back to my hotel room and keep an eye on Cray. Do moths have a choice of flame?

We talk for a bit. Jessica's from Duluth. She's in town for a conference, has never been in Memphis before. She has a quiet sense of humor.

"Really liked hearing you play." She reaches out her hand and I feel its gentle weight on mine for a moment.

"Thanks," I say.

She smiles but all I see is the big rock. I imagine what she's got stashed in her jewelry drawer back home, and what the money could mean to someone who needed it.

"Do you know him?" Jessica asks, suddenly serious.

I assume this question has to do with God. We're in Bible country here. "I believe in a higher power, if that's what you mean," I say carefully. "I'm not sure I think of it as a Him, or even anything that . . ."

"No," she says firmly, pointing behind my shoulder. "Do you know *him*?"

There, a couple of tables away, sits Cray, blowing kisses at us.

"That's my nephew," I say. "He's traveling with me, kind of."

"He looks strange."

"He is." Given his heritage, he never had a chance at normal.

"What's his problem?"

"He's mental and his meds aren't working."

"I work for a drug company. Maybe I can help." She smiles. "We get samples, you know."

"He needs more than a sample."

Cray orders a beer, hands the waiter a twenty.

"I think I have to go," I say, reluctantly. "When he drinks, it's not pretty."

"Maybe we can get back together after you medicate him and tuck him in." She writes her room number on a napkin and hands it to me. "I have a Merck Manual. You could read him a bedtime story."

"He's not really crazy, just malnourished. Living on burritos."

She gives a broad, honest smile. "You're nice to let him travel with you. He doesn't know how lucky he is."

"Really, why?"

"Because you look like you're fun to be around." She sidles up and kisses me awkwardly.

"You'd have to ask him about that."

Jessica downs a glass of white wine with an audible glug. "What's his name?"

"Cray."

"That's strange."

"It's from Cray Research. They made the first supercomputers. My brother is a big fan of technology."

"What does he do?"

"He's a . . . printer."

Jessica's eyes unfocus for a moment and I'm afraid she's going to keel. But she rallies.

"I really like talking to you," she whispers. "Come up to my room later, promise?"

"Yes. Absolutely." I stand up and lean forward to kiss her on her lips, neck, and finally, her earlobe—one of my favorite places—which triggers a low gasp. I feel nothing; my patented moves are as counterfeit as Ray's twenties. Jessica meanders off.

"What about my beer?" Cray asks as I lift him up from his chair and shove him toward the door. "I paid for it."

"With real money?"

"No. Of course not."

"Then let someone else have it. A little sharing never hurt anyone."

We leave the bar and Cray straightens his jacket. He's wearing my suit again.

"You promised me a couple of beers."

"You can drink them in the room."

"Boring," he mutters. "Hey, who was that drunk chick you were talking to?"

"An old friend," I lie. "From college."

"No way. Like your girlfriend or something?"

"Yes."

"Well don't let me interfere."

"You already did." I press the elevator's call button.

We watch the elevator lights move upward. The door opens at the seventh floor and Cray and I walk down the long carpeted hallway past the ice machine room, the linen closets with all the items necessary to keep guests happy—miniature plastic bottles of shampoo, conditioner, mouthwash.

In the room, Cray retrieves his contractual Amstel Lights from the minibar and clicks the television on to a show about people who eat progressively disgusting things. A woman in a tank top stabs a plastic fork into a plate of fried cicadas.

"I'm going out for a bit."

"College reunion?" He winces as the reluctant gourmand gags and turns to the side to spray the ground with her lunch.

"Don't wait up."

"Are your intentions honorable?" Cray intones in a fatherly voice.

I pick up my fakebook. "No, they're not."

"Go for it, Uncle Ross," he says. "I was getting worried that you were too good. Anyone who eats miso soup for breakfast is worrisome to me."

"Better than cicadas."

"Yes, but not as good as bacon and eggs."

"Debatable."

Cray covers his face with his hands, then peers out between his fingers to watch a burly guy eat scorpions dipped in chocolate.

"So, you going to be okay?" I ask.

"I might hurl if this keeps up."

"I mean being alone in the hotel room."

"Uncle Ross, I'm used to it. Dad's always out in the barn. I like being alone."

"You sure?"

"Yes. Go off and spawn like a mighty king salmon."

"That's not what I have in mind."

Cray drank the last swig of Amstel Light, opened another. "Then burn a beeswax candle and read the freaking Kabbalah together until you achieve mutual enlightenment. What-fucking-ever."

I laugh, leave Cray in the room, convinced that he's up to something, but not sure what it is.

Jessica's wearing a hotel-issued plush white robe when I knock on her door. It's good to be back in the diamond business again.

"I thought you'd never get here," she says coyly, waving me in. Her blond hair is wet, skin still flushed from the bath. Her room is identical to ours except the two twin beds have been replaced with a king-sized one with a blue bedspread. On it are Jessica's magazines, laptop, and cell phone—all the essential elements of the lonely traveler. We sit on the edge of the bed.

"I had to spend a little time with my nephew."

She hands me a glass of wine from the bedside table. "Your sister's son?"

"No, my brother's."

"Do you get along with your brother?"

"Good question." I pause. "We're alike but pretty different."

"Was he nice to you when you were kids?"

I shrug. "He was older. So I was always kind of annoying to him."

"But he wasn't mean to you, was he? Never beat you up."

I pause at this odd question, watch Jessica gulp her wine. We're stumbling into a cave and she's leading the way. "No, he never beat me up. Did yours?"

She nods, then pulls one side of her robe slowly down her arm. An irregular dark splotch, crosshatched by a tiny line of stitches, marks her upper arm like a tattoo. "My stepbrother really hated me. Broke my arm once. Pushed me off my bike when I was eleven. The bone stuck out here."

"That's terrible."

"That's not the half of it."

I take the hint. "What else?"

She shakes her head. "You don't want to know."

"I do."

Jessica starts to cry, tears rolling down her cheeks suddenly. "When I was fifteen, he snuck into my room one night." She bites her lower lip, looks down at the carpet. "He was strong and pulled my legs apart with his knee, bit me on the neck, and raped me until I passed out. I was bleeding. My first time and I'm raped by my own stepbrother—they wonder at work why I don't have a boyfriend."

Jessica pulls her arm back and sends her wineglass whistling across the room with a powerful throw worthy of Vuckovich, my favorite White Sox pitcher. It shatters on the wall, spraying shards down on the sofa, the coffee table.

I say nothing, just shake my head. I run my fingers along Jessica's leg, then sit on the bed next to her.

She pulls away.

"Did you tell your parents?"

"Not right away. But later."

"What happened?"

"They made him join the Army. He stayed in long enough for me to get out of the house and go to college. Then he joined the National Guard when he came back—now here's the really sick part." She shakes her head. "I mean, it's like the kind of story people tell you and you don't believe it. You think they're just bullshitting you. But I'm telling the truth, uh . . ."

"Ross," I say.

"Ross, I'm serious about this part. There's no reason for me to make anything up, is there?"

"No, there's not," I say.

"Anyway, he's in the Guard for a while. Then Bush comes around and he gets called up for active duty. First week in Baghdad, a grenade comes through the window of his Humvee and lands right in his lap. It blows him into little pieces. God was getting revenge for me. They didn't even bother trying to send anything home. No body bag. Nothing but a flag. I took the day off work when I heard the news. Drank a bottle of tequila and watched CNN. Saw the report about his patrol. But it didn't make me feel good. How can you feel good about anyone getting killed, even someone terrible?"

"You can't."

"No way," Jessica says, her flat Minnesota accent stretching out every word like a snowy field. She waves her glass in front of her. "I didn't finish my story. After Garrett gets blown away, suddenly he's a hero. They rename a street for him. They put all his medals in a case in the high school. Now anytime I bad-mouth him, they tell me I'm being unpatriotic. Can you believe that?"

"Yes, I can."

She shakes her head. "I can't believe I told you all this. I never even tell people at work about it. It's ancient history."

"Maybe not."

Jessica cradles her head in her hands; tears darken the shiny bedspread. I watch the diamond shimmering on her right hand. I put my arm around Jessica, slip my hand beneath her robe to touch her warm back.

She closes her eyes and shivers slightly. "It's been a really long time since someone touched me. I'm not sure I remember how to do it."

I look into her bloodshot brown eyes. "You don't have to."

She nods, lets the robe fall from her shoulders, and lies back on the bed. I open the robe and touch the line of stitches on her arm, press it gently. I run my fingers up to her lips and touch them, feel her kiss my fingertips. I go to work with the diligence of an explorer, improvising along the unique terrain of Jessica, a woman with nothing to lose but her suspicion, her sadness, her diamond.

———

I kneel next to the bed, wearing only my black trousers, flashlight in my mouth, calipers ready as I maneuver Jessica's "me" hand out from beneath the covers. I lift it carefully and move closer, magnifier twisted tightly in my eye. Live diamond theft can be tricky. In West Palm Beach, I once removed a pair of three-carat diamond studs from a sleeping real estate broker with my tongue. In Montreal, I plucked an engagement stone from its setting while its owner writhed beneath my other hand. A gift, some might say.

The diamond looks very good. Over two carats, fine clarity, the cut straight and clean. One squeeze from the calipers and it falls into my hand.

I hear tapping. Jessica stirs. I look around the dim suite, see nothing but the TV flickering in the living room.

The tapping starts again, louder.

A thin man stands motionless on the narrow balcony outside the window, hands pressed against the glass just a few feet from me. Dressed in black, he wears a ski mask. My stomach drops.

I freeze for a second, then let everything drop silently to the carpet—the magnifier, the calipers, my flashlight, the diamond.

We stare at each other for a moment, two thieves meeting in the night, impossibly bad timing for us both. I only wanted a diamond. Maybe all he wanted was a sleeping woman. I look around the room for something to defend Jessica with, but see only clothes strewn on the floor.

The man pulls up the ski mask to reveal a wide grin and gleaming eyes.

I want to scream at Cray but can't without waking Jessica, whose outstretched hand pokes from beneath the covers, her ring's gaping setting begging for its diamond back. I point furiously toward the living room and Cray nods, pads carefully across the balcony.

Jessica opens her eyes to narrow slits, sees me standing next to the bed. "You okay?"

"Fine," I say. "I'm just going to get some water."

Her head falls heavily back on her pillow and she groans. "Bring me some too, will you? My head hurts."

"Sure. Be right back."

I walk to the living room and open the door to the balcony carefully. Cray steps in, smiling, as if I should be very glad to see him.

"What the hell are you doing sneaking around outside?" I whisper.

"Exploring," Cray says.

"Exploring what?"

"The outside of the hotel. I told you I like rock climbing. Did you know it's really easy to climb up and down these balconies? You don't even need a rope."

"No, I didn't know that. How did you find me?"

"I figured it out."

"How long were you standing in the bedroom window?"

"I missed the fireworks, but got to see the sparks," Cray says. "Is it nice to steal your girlfriend's diamond?"

"She's not really my girlfriend."

"Is it nice to steal anyone's diamond?"

"No, but . . ."

"But what?"

"But go away," I hiss at Cray, stabbing at him with my index finger. "We'll talk about it in the morning."

Jessica stirs in the bedroom. "Ross, you coming back?" she slurs.

"Yes, be right there," I holler back toward the bedroom.

Cray pulls his ski mask back on and steps out on the balcony.

"No, Spider-Man." I pull him back inside and push him toward the door. "Take the elevator."

"Okay, okay," he says. "You are so bossy."

I shut the door quietly and fill a glass of water at the sink, then slip back into the bedroom, climb back into bed.

"Do you have to leave so soon?" Jessica reaches her arm around me and pulls me closer, presses her cheek against my chest.

"In a bit."

"Stay just a little longer. Until I fall asleep."

"I will." I lie still, thinking of how Cray has to go home, and wait for Jessica's breathing to slow.

Cray and I sit silently at the breakfast table the next morning while our waitress circles, trying to keep every piece of glassware in front of us full of fluids—coffee, ice water, orange juice.

When she's on the other side of the hotel restaurant, I bend toward Cray. "Do you know how much trouble you almost got us into?"

Cray pulls off his headphones. "What?"

I stab my finger at him. "Do you know how much trouble you almost got us into?"

He shrugs. "Us? I wasn't doing anything wrong."

"You could have fallen off the balcony," I say. "Or you could have been arrested. Either way, it would have been a real problem for both of us."

"What about you, Uncle Ross? You think stealing a diamond isn't a real problem?"

"That wasn't what I was doing."

"Looked like it to me."

"There's more to it than that."

"Sure." Cray shakes his head slowly. "Whatever you say."

"I'll tell you about it."

"When?"

"Later, when I'm not so mad at you that I want to call Ray and have him pick you up."

"Don't do that, Uncle Ross."

Cray doesn't want to go home, and I can't really blame him. "I won't. But you've got to promise me one thing, Cray."

"What's that?"

"You won't mention last night to anyone. Not even Ray. And you won't do anything else to get in trouble."

"That's actually two promises, Uncle Ross."

"What?"

"You said I had to promise one thing."

I raise my hands. "That's it. I'm calling Ray after breakfast."

"Good luck with that. Even I don't know how to call him." Cray pours a box of Frosted Flakes into his bowl, douses them with milk. "Like it or not, you're stuck with me."

"I don't like it at all."

Cray stops for a moment, lowers his face toward the table-cloth. His shoulders start to shake. When he raises his face, it's streaked with tears.

"Stop it!" I throw a napkin at him.

Cray shrugs, wipes his face. "Worth a try."

"I'm on to your tricks, Cray."

"And I'm on to yours, Uncle Ross." He looks both ways, then leans forward over his cereal bowl. "Stealing diamonds is so old-fashioned. Maybe you should hold up stagecoaches or some-thing. You know, on a freaking white horse."

I realize that Cray doesn't really have a problem with my stealing. I just chose to steal something amazingly *retro*. "So what should I be stealing, Cray?"

He shrugs. "I don't know. Intellectual property." He smiles broadly, remembering something. "Anyway, you should see what people do in hotel rooms. It's better than porno, Uncle Ross. I saw a prom night fleshpile, nurses stripping, a couple of hookers . . ."

"Really?"

Cray rolls his eyes. "No, Uncle Ross. You really are the most gullible person in the world. I saw people watching TV, sitting at their computers, talking on their cell phones. No good parts at all. Makes your lame-o diamond heist seem exciting. Wait until Dad hears about it. He won't believe it—you stealing something. You must be hurting for money."

My face turns hot. "No, I am not hurting for money. And I told you that you couldn't mention this to anyone. Particularly not Ray."

"Oh yeah, that was one of the promises. I remember now." He nods. "But I'm not that good with secrets." He brings a drip-ping spoonful of cereal to his mouth.

To be alone again would be heaven. I promise myself never to complain about being lonely.

"I've been thinking, though," Cray says, putting down his spoon. "I'm a pretty good climber. I could do the outside part and get you in almost anyone's room. There's probably lots of people with some fine jewelry staying in hotels. We could be a team."

I stop for a moment, resist the urge to press my grapefruit half into my nephew's face, Jimmy Cagney–like.

"So what do you think?"

"I don't think so, Cray. I'm just not . . ."

"Not what?"

"Not that interested. Let's leave it at that."

He pushes away from the breakfast table. "Be that way," he says. "But just forget about me helping you. From here on in, we're just traveling together. Nothing else. I won't get in any trouble or mess up your little routine. You can be as boring as you want to be."

I nod.

"I'll see you tonight, maybe," he says.

"Where're you going?"

"I'm going to have some fun. I haven't had any since I met up with you." Cray tosses a couple of twenties on the table, then holds up his roll. "I'm going to spend this and then some. I'm going to meet some really fine girls, not the so-called ladies you hang out with, the sad drunk ones with problems. And I'll promise you one thing."

"What's that?"

"I won't steal anything from them," he whispers, then puts on his black raincoat and walks quickly through the restaurant, winding around the tables and the fake potted plants like an errant cloud.

I play the second night of the two-night gig on *auto-pianist*, running through my set list song by song, note for note. I look out for Jessica but she's gone, returned to Duluth with a hangover and a fake diamond. After Malcolm, Cray is the first person to know that I steal diamonds, news that has left him less than impressed. I can't put much faith in his reaction. Still, I seem to have let Cray down somehow. And more—I'm worried what kind of trouble he might be getting into, spewing counterfeit twenties like an ATM on meth.

There are diamonds in the audience, throwing sparks along the ceiling when a hand hovers near a candle. But I don't pursue them. Instead, I go up to our hotel room, glaringly absent of Cray and all the chaos and mess that he generates. It's peaceful and boring. I lie in bed, hear only the low roar, like a seashell held to the ear, that comes after every gig—the accumulated sonic debris of bass chords, fast melodies, the voices of strangers. All reverberating in my head.

During the months after I met Delmar, I played our spinet hard and fast, hoping that somewhere inside its phony ornate white-and-gold shell its stringy guts would break so we would have to buy a real piano. Chief walked in and I expected him to tell me to cut it out.

"Ross, there's an old black man out front who says he wants to see you," he said instead.

Outside, I found Delmar in his deep brown Mercury with its shredded brougham roof held together with strips of silver duct tape. He took off his wraparound Ray-Bans when I came out of the house and stood on the sidewalk between two cement planters.

"Ross, baby," Delmar said slowly. "Sorry to intrude."

"You're not."

"Come to say goodbye."

I tried to summon up my nightclub gaze, direct and cool. But I was standing in front of my parents' faux colonial dream home in Lake Forest. "So where're you going?"

"Detroit. I got a sweet deal going there. Three nights head-lining, free apartment, the works."

I nodded.

Delmar reached through the open window of his car and took out a green plastic binder. "I was cleaning up and I found this. It's my old one—don't need it no more. Thought you might have use for it."

The fakebook held scrawled charts ringed with wine stains, pencil marks, phone numbers, signatures, dates, club names, women's names. There were hundreds of pages of subterranean codex, songs I had always wanted to play and some I had never heard of. Even in a glance I saw the names of my early saints—Monk, Oscar Peterson, Erroll Garner, Red Garland, Tadd Dameron, Bill Evans.

"Thanks, Delmar," I said. "I mean it." That's all I could come up with. Melodies were my strong point, not words.

Delmar nodded, put his shades back on. "How about some folding money for gas, then?"

I took out my wallet and handed him all the cash.

"Thank you, young gentleman." He got into the Mercury and slammed the door. "You got a gift, keep on working at it," he said. "You could be like old Delmar someday, driving off to a sweet gig in Detroit." He smiled and hit the gas, spraying gravel into the lawn as he sped off. I kicked gravel back over the tire marks, knowing I'd hear about it from Chief if I didn't.

I found out a few weeks later that Delmar wasn't racing off to Detroit. He was going to his sister's house in Skokie to hide from a child-support warrant and gambling debts. He wasn't the first to dream up a sunny future of sweet gigs. Three months later, my nightlife *passeur* would be dead, overdosed in his car at a stoplight, cars honking behind him for miles.

I heard about it at the Top Spot between sets, went out in the ratty alley to cry.

The phone rings long after midnight. I click the lamp on, reach clumsily for the receiver.

"Hello?" I listen for a moment, wonder who would call this late, hope it isn't Cray.

"UNCLE ROSS," Cray shouts.

"Are you okay?" I envision hospitals, police stations.

"Fine, never better."

I cover my eyes to shield them from the table lamp. "Why aren't you back?" I look at the digital clock radio. "It's almost two."

"You busy?"

"Busy?"

"You know. Stealing more diamonds from your college girl-friend or some other lady."

"I was asleep, Cray. Is this an emergency?"

"KIND OF," he shouts.

"Can it wait? I mean, you didn't fall off a balcony. You're not bleeding, are you?"

"No, no falling, no blood. Just meet me in the lobby. Quick like a bunny."

"Hold on," I say, but the phone clicks and Cray is gone. I fling the phone over on the couch. Then I toss the covers off and pull on my clothes.

Cray stands in the center of the lobby, bouncing from one foot to the other, hooded sweatshirt pulled over his head, mirrored sunglasses firmly in place. The desk clerk tries to will him away from the hotel with a hard stare. Still half-asleep, I don't look any more respectable.

"What's wrong?"

Cray grabs my sleeve and pulls me toward the door. "Nothing. It's just we don't have much time."

"For what."

"For fun."

"I was already having fun."

Cray's eyes narrow suspiciously. "You were having sex."

"No, I was asleep, by myself. Sometimes that's my idea of fun."

"Then you've got a problem, Uncle Ross, because that college friend of yours had the *look of love* in her eyes last night."

"More like the look of chardonnay. Anyway, she's gone."

"Good, then we're ready for Boys' Night Out. Come on, it's this way," he says. "I think they close at three."

Cray leads me down a side street, across a parking lot, and down a wide alley. A neon sign sputters before the alley turns into a row of Dumpsters. The White Sands.

"I'm not buying you a drink. You're already acting strange. Have you been snorting Pixy Stix or something?"

Cray gives me a hurt look. "I haven't even had a beer. They won't serve me here, if you can believe it. Sticklers about the law. So I've had six of those energy drinks, the ones that come in little silver cans? I'm feeling a little weird, I got to tell you."

"Oh no."

We walk into the crowded bar. On a tiny stage, a black man sits in a chair and plays tenor sax, a young Asian kid plucks a battered upright bass that dwarfs him, and a long-haired guy of indeterminate age strums an electric guitar and stares at his shoeless feet. Tucked at the back of the stage, the drummer drinks, smokes, and plays drums, almost at the same time.

"HEY!" Cray shouts at the top of his lungs. Failing to quiet the roar of the bar, he sticks two fingers in his mouth and emits a whistling shriek louder than the Emergency Broadcast System. The room falls silent and wary eyes settle on us.

"HEY GUYS! THIS IS MY UNCLE! THE ONE I TOLD YOU ABOUT." Cray's neck bulges with veins and his face turns crimson. "HE'S A GREAT PIANO PLAYER. YOU'RE LUCKY TO HAVE HIM HERE IN THIS DUMP."

The room turns silent. The crowd seems to edge toward us a bit. In France in the fifties, they would have called this place *une boîte,* charming and hip, the kind of place Dizzy Gillespie would have dropped by at midnight and stayed until dawn. But here in Memphis, Cray is right. It's no Minton's. It's just another dumpy bar with live music, sort of.

"IT'S OPEN MIKE NIGHT, RIGHT?" Cray hollers.

No response.

I size up the crowd for a moment. A mix of neighborhood types, probably not that glad to see a stranger in a dark suit stepping into their bar. I could turn around, walk back to the hotel, and go back to sleep. But I decide to get through my nephew's latest mess like a pro.

"My name's Ross Clifton," I say. "I play piano. I'm going to sit in for a little bit. But first, have a round of drinks on me while we figure out what we're going to play."

The crowd cheers and rushes toward the bar. I know a trick or two about getting over.

"Feel like putting a stack of Jacksons into circulation?" I whisper to Cray.

"Sure." He smiles, heads toward the bar.

I climb up on the low stage, play a quick scale on the upright piano, find it sounds okay considering it's in a back-alley bar somewhere in Memphis.

"You play jazz?" the shoeless guitar player asks.

I nod.

"You know *Moondance*?" Everyone laughs, then gathers around the piano to hear me start up, a brief run from *Spiral,* a John Coltrane number that's always overshadowed by *Giant Steps,* then a bit of *In Walked Bud,* the Monk standard.

We shake hands, pass along the basic information that will let us do a set together. Yuji, the bass player, is in college and just getting into jazz. The sax player, Lafon Washington III, played in a touring soul act for five years. Now he plays in a lounge called the Timber Inn, and comes by for open mike night because the beer is cheaper here. Lafon has beautiful hands, fingers tapered and annealed to pink at the tips, and as he tells me his story, his fingers run across the saxophone involuntarily, as if they were intended to do only that. I'm hopeful.

The guitar player, Jimmy, is a session player—mostly jingles, no shame in that—who used to tour in a rock band that we'd all recognize except that he's legally prohibited from even mentioning its name. I'm dubious about Jimmy, but he's playing a nice Gibson hollow body. As he tells his tale, he doesn't look at me, just burns out compact riffs that sound okay and not particularly loud.

The drummer, Clem, sits behind a dinky Gretsch cocktail kit, tightening his battered snare with a butter knife. He doesn't even get up.

We get down to business. "How about four songs, one eight-bar solo for each of us, two on the last number?"

They nod.

"You was playing Coltrane before," Lafon mutters, pulling his mouth off his reed for a moment. "You know *A Love Supreme*?"

"I do, Lafon," I say. "But we're not playing that. It's way too long, and there's chanting."

He smiles. It's clear that the other guys are happy just to let Lafon and me sort out the set list. They're sidemen. Too many leaders make for a very messy band. Consider Miles Davis's stint with the Ellington band, Monk's rough months with Miles, or Jimi Hendrix's time with James Brown. There are leaders and followers, and the best band involves fewer of the former and more of the latter.

"How about we start with *'Round Midnight*," Lafon says. "Everybody know that one?"

The others nod.

"Then we could do *Straight, No Chaser* to pick it up a bit," I volunteer, knowing where Lafon's going with this set list. Nice sax solos, the Charlie Rouse kind that grab the spotlight.

Again, universal agreement. When musicians aren't getting paid, they're remarkably easy to deal with. Besides, our audience is less than discerning. They're drinking Schlitz and cherry brandy on the rocks, from what I can tell.

"You guys know any Mose Allison?" Yuji asks. "I just bought one of his records at a yard sale."

We nod. Mutual admiration for Mose, a saint in almost everyone's fakebook. "How about we do his take on *Do Nothin' Till You Hear From Me*?" Lafon asks.

"Fine by me," I say. "One of my favorites."

"You know the words?" Lafon asks. "'Cause you'll be singing it. It's got some fine words. You a singer too?"

"Sure," I say. "Why not."

"Yes indeedy, why not. Fine night for a singing." Lafon signals the bartender for his free drink.

"And to finish, how about *All Blues*?" I ask. "We can stretch it out if you want."

More nods, then we huddle over the charts for a few minutes, lost in the minutia. We might as well have been printers looking over a proof, bankers lost in a balance sheet. Every trade has its thatch of details and being a musician is no different. Chord charts. Intros. Ordering the solos—sax, guitar, bass, drums. Setting the tempo. Working out the signals and glances, the semaphores of clubland. Figuring out how to end gracefully.

The free drinks are already gone and Cray's waving frantically from the bar. I nod, then look over at the "band" for a moment before I start to play the expansive intro to 'Round Midnight. Clem appears to be sleeping now, a thin thread of drool connecting the corner of his mouth to the floor. Lafon's standing right next to the upright in imitation of the classic sax player stance, nestled in the curve of the grand piano. This piano being less than grand—cigarette burns mark almost every key—he stands to my left, his drink on the piano lid.

Lafon turns and gives Clem a gentle kick. "Hey. Hey, Clem. Showtime, baby." Clem reaches down and picks up his brushes, then gives me a nod, ready to go. A glance circles our little ad hoc quintet and I play the first notes.

For the first two numbers, Cray jitters around in front of the crowd, which perks up now—from the free drinks or the music, who can say? But by the Mose Allison number, my coat is off, sleeves rolled up. Sweat is dripping down our faces—even long after midnight, the club is steaming with early summer heat.

"Do nothin' till you hear from me," I all but shout. We're

playing this old chestnut as fast as I've ever heard it. Somewhere Duke Ellington is revolving elegantly in his grave. *"Pay no attention to what's said."* A shout from Lafon here. *"Why people tear the seams of anyone's dream . . . is over my head."*

The crowd starts to cheer and doesn't let up until the song's over. They're dancing in front of the stage, Cray included, swerving around with a pierced girl in a plaid shirt. Maybe they recognize some part of the melody from their childhoods, their parents' records, the radio when they were younger. For whatever reason, this song unlocks the crowd like a long-lost key and they cheer and shout as if our quintet of strangers is made up of returning heroes. Jimmy takes a tasteful guitar solo, a smart Joe Pass reference in the middle. Then he keeps going and going—eight bars, twelve bars, and beyond.

Lafon and I look at each other. Jimmy is a showboat, stealing measure after measure until Clem realizes what's going on and shuts him down with four bars of lock-step drum fills—this from someone who was almost comatose half an hour ago.

We bow, then while they're still clapping, Yuji starts the rolling bass figure that marks the beginning of *All Blues*. The incantatory power of this song is hard to describe. In the jazz hymnal, it's at the top. Lafon's playing the trumpet leads on a throaty sax, taking it down into the gutter. But in a good way. I look over and watch Cray leading a long line of people up a bar stool and along the bar, doing a dance that involves raising their fingertips toward the sweating ceiling, then lowering them to the floor.

My solo comes up.

My hands move of their own volition, hitting new chords, improvising melodies that only hint at their source. I smile, lost in my eight bars. Imagine for a moment that you can do whatever you want with complete freedom. At the seventh bar, I nod at Lafon and get permission to take another eight. I raise the volume and pull the move Delmar taught me. I play four bars, lowering down toward the keyboard in a crouch, then rise up, playing the figure backward. Time reverses.

The crowd screams. I knock back the piano stool and pound the last chords, the others joining in to make a pure ending that sustains for a moment, then fades, replaced by cheering.

The band takes a deep bow, then puts their instruments on the ground and rushes to the bar through a gauntlet of backslaps and handshakes. Cray wanders up to the edge of the stage and finds me sitting on a guitar case, head low, sweat dripping from my face.

Cray just shakes his head, then shouts at me, "THAT WAS INCREDIBLE" and I should "PLAY WITH A BAND MORE INSTEAD OF DOING THAT SMARMY HOTEL SHIT."

Cray quiets for a moment and squints at Clem, pale and slumped over his drum kit. "Hey, is that dude okay?"

"I think so." I lean over and give Clem a kick and he comes to life again, sending out a short drumroll before collapsing slowly to the floor.

Lafon saunters up. "I seen him do this before. He's taking some medication that makes him kind of dizzy sometimes."

We huddle over Clem, shake him until he pinks up a bit, then I tuck $100 into his jacket pocket when no one's looking, plus $100 in Lafon's sax case, and walk back through the crowd, Cray trailing me. I stop and scan the crowd, realize that I'm looking for Marianne London, unlikely in an after-hours club. There are only drunk strangers, who reach out to touch me like a totem.

We make our way back through the alley and into the night. Above us, the stars wheel along their paths, beautiful but indifferent. Our time on stage is over, fading already, then gone forever. I shiver in the cooling night air, steam rising from my shoulders.

"It was . . ." Cray fails to summon up an adjective.

I say nothing, just lead us back to where our quiet hotel room waits.

Cray reaches out and stops me. "You ought to play like that all the time, man. Not all that . . ." He wiggles his fingers in the air. "You know, that boring stuff. Do you really like it?"

I shrug. "It's not about liking it or not liking it anymore. It's just what I ended up learning how to play, and what I got good at. If I had picked up cello instead of piano, maybe I'd be playing Brahms in an orchestra. Or playing guitar in a rock band. It's all pretty much the same."

"Then maybe you should do something different."

"Like what?"

"I don't know." Cray's yellow hair is sweat-crusted and spiky beneath his hooded sweatshirt. "Like wilder."

"Wilder than what?"

Cray shrugs. "Than the usual boring stuff that people do every day."

"How about this." I reach into my pocket for the Dealer Master Key, point it at a silver L-Series sedan. The locks click open. "Hop in."

"I didn't know you had a BMW," Cray says.

"I don't." I pop in the key and start the engine with a roar, then pull out.

"Where we going?"

"For a wild drive." We drive east, away from downtown.

Cray touches the gleaming wood inlaid in the dashboard. "This is one nice car, Uncle Ross, where'd you get it?"

"You saw where I got it. Off Union Avenue."

Cray squints for a moment, pulls off his silver headphones. "So you're stealing this car, Uncle Ross?"

I nod. "I'm stealing this car, Cray."

"Just like that?"

"Just like that."

"Wait until I tell Dad. First you're stealing diamonds, then you're stealing cars . . . what next?"

"Whoa. I'm not sure your Dad needs to know about all this."

"Okay, okay." Cray holds up his hands then rests them on the dashboard. He pulls them away quickly. "Guess I better not touch anything, right?"

"Don't worry, they'll take care of it."

"They?"

"The . . . distributors, I guess you could call them." I drive down Poplar, looking for an address Malcolm had e-mailed me earlier. It's an old garage with a rusted pump out front. I pull in.

"Stopping for gas? The gauge says there's plenty," Cray says.

I honk three times and the door slides open. We drive in and it shuts behind us.

"Get out and don't say anything."

An older man in a rumpled seersucker suit peers at the car with a flashlight, checks under the hood, in the wheel wells.

"You're working kind of late," he says.

"Never know when opportunity will knock."

Cray stands by me, shifting from one foot to the other.

"Who you got with you?"

"A helper."

"Might want to tell him not to dress like a punk. Makes it easier to get caught." The man smiles, then hands me an envelope. "Six thousand."

I nod. "Pleasure doing business with you."

He opens a small door at the side of the shop and holds it open for us. "The pleasure, friends, was all mine."

Less than a minute after arriving, we find ourselves out on the street, the first pale blue marks of the sun along the eastern skyline.

We walk. "What the hell was that?" Cray says after a while.

"A business transaction." I tell him about China's insatiable craving for BMWs. I give him an introduction to the DMK and its miraculous sonic workings. I tell him about the fee scale for BMWs, about the various classes and models. But I don't tell him what I do with the money.

"Wow," Cray says, pulling down his hood to run his fingers through his hair. He seems stunned. "It's really weird, Uncle Ross, I always thought you were just out there tickling the ivories at hotels. I thought Dad was the one doing something . . . subversive, like he likes to call it." He pauses, shakes his head. "I mean, it's pretty strange when you get an idea in your head and then you find out it's all wrong."

"Believe me, it won't be the last time," I say.

"I think my energy drinks just wore off. I need to go to sleep."

"Not for too long. We need to be on the road by nine."

Cray stops and squints at me. "I take back what I said this morning. I'm having an okay time."

"I am too, Cray, kind of."

We walk east toward the hotel, tired and sweaty, an unlikely duo coursing through the gray city before sunrise. A newspaper truck roars by, while above us city crows grip telephone lines, their gleaming black eyes alone marking our passage through Memphis.

louisville

A late night of car theft has reinvigorated Cray. He's jabbering about ridding the world of BMWs. He wants his own DMK, wonders if there's one for Mercedes, his favorite brand.

The highway is crowded with travelers and Cray amuses himself (and to a much lesser degree, me) with one of his favorite pastimes.

"There goes a Ford Fucktard!" he blurts out, then hunches over and laughs so hard his headphones fall off.

He points. "And look, there's the brand-new Chevy Scrotum! Seats two, get it?"

"I get it, Cray."

"And the Chrysler Merkin. Know what that is?" Cray twitches like a hidden demon is poking him with pins.

"Yes, thanks for that."

"Come up with your own, then."

I point. "There's a Dodge Downturn, the car you used to be able to afford but can't now."

"Nice. You would come up with that one, Major Buzzkill."

Cray dozes off finally, talking himself into sleep like a dog chasing its own tail. The car reverts to blessed quiet. We turn off on a state highway that winds past weathered farmhouses, collapsed barns, gray fences, and cattle huddled in the shade. Even through my closed window, an insistent chorus of cicadas oscillates. We pass through a verdant leaf tunnel, ash trees rippling in our wake. The leaves silver for a moment, then turn green again. The road brightens as the woods give way to tobacco fields and open pastures.

I slam on the brakes.

Cray wakes and stares, wide-eyed. *"Whoa."*

Ahead, black skid marks end in a steaming wreck. A silver pickup truck is flipped upside down in the center of the road, wheels still spinning.

We pull over by the side of the road.

"You stay here for a minute," I say. "Call 911. Tell them we're on Route 100, about ten miles south of Centerville. Get them to send an ambulance."

Cray nods, takes out his cell phone.

I run toward the truck, stepping through broken glass and pieces of plastic and chrome. A tan, short-haired dog rises from the weeds by the side of the road and growls at me. It tries to stand but its legs buckle. Its snout is bloodied and one flank is scraped down to slick pink skin.

The debris thickens near the truck. A white lump, shiny as soap, sits on a neat square of denim. As I walk closer, I see that it's a kneecap. I look away, take a deep breath of gasoline-tainted air.

I kneel and look inside the cab of the overturned pickup, find a farmer hanging head-down by his seat belt, crushed between the seat and the steering column. His face is tanned and creased as leather, blue eyes wide open, scalp peeled back from smashing into the windshield, a spiderweb of cracks now. I feel his neck, the skin loose and cool to my touch. No pulse. Papers blow in a circle on the ceiling, now the floor. Receipts, food wrappers, pages from a seed catalog—the farmer's blood marks them all with thick red drops.

"Uncle Ross?" I look up and see Cray, pale and shaking. "I can't get my cell phone to work. We're in the middle of fucking nowhere."

"You sure?"

"I tried over and over. Is that guy dead?"

"Yes."

"Old MacDonald bought the farm," Cray whispers reverently. He makes a version of the Sign of the Cross, then shivers uncontrollably.

"Looks like he hit that car." Down the hillside, a white sedan has rolled over and over, coming to rest sideways in a creekbed. "We should go see if they're all right."

We hear sirens in the distance.

"I think we'd better get out of here, Uncle Ross," Cray says. "I don't feel like explaining why I've got ten thousand dollars in counterfeit twenties in my backpack. And I think you're probably holding a few diamonds, am I right?"

I nod. "Let's get going." We walk toward our car, past the half-skinned dog, sprawled in the weeds now, flies on its heaving flank.

Cray looks away.

The dog's ears perk up and it tries to stand but can't. I reach down and rub its speckled nose. It licks my fingers.

"Come on, Uncle Ross," Cray says.

Cray jumps in the car, anxious to drive on, to leave the dangling farmer, the white car in the beautiful creek, the dying dog.

Twenty miles later we stop at a Waffle House and I run tepid water over my hands in the bathroom to wash away the morning. When I walk back into the restaurant, Cray is sitting in a corner booth, head down.

"That was just too . . . too fucking *real*." He runs his fingers through his hair. "I mean, if I want to see shit like that, Uncle Ross, I'll turn on the television and watch *Hillbilly 911*." He opens a packet of sugar and eats it, then another.

I say nothing.

The waitress comes and we order iced teas.

"You think they're all dead?"

"Maybe the dog will live, but I doubt it."

"All because someone crossed a few inches into the wrong lane?"

"Something like that."

"Could have been us, you know." Cray's eyes widen. "A couple of minutes earlier and we could have been the ones that smacked into that truck head-on."

"That's true."

Cray rubs his forehead. "You're not exactly making me feel better, Uncle Ross." Our iced teas arrive and Cray stirs in four sugars.

"Why should I make you feel better? This isn't about you, Cray. Some people just died on the road and we're drinking iced tea at a Waffle House. Just be glad to be alive."

"I am, I guess," he says. "But I feel bad now, really bad."

"Of course you do. You probably wish you could have done something to save them, but you couldn't. And that makes you feel kind of helpless."

"That's part of it," he says. "But mostly I just feel bad that it happened at all. And that we had to be the ones right behind it and see it."

"People get shot, die of cancer, lose their children, watch their houses burn. Just because we can't see it all doesn't mean it's not happening every day."

Cray stares at me for a moment. "Dad's right about you."

"How's that?"

He shakes his head. "I'm not saying."

"I assume that means it isn't good."

"Depends on what you mean by good."

I say nothing. Cray puts his thumb over the end of his straw and pulls it out, then dribbles the tea back into the glass. He does it again.

"He said you were always more worried about other people than your own family."

"What's that supposed to mean?"

Cray lets the straw drift back into the tea. "How am I supposed to know?"

I think about it for a moment, realize I don't really want to hear the truth, at least Ray's version of it. I take a drink of tea. "Heard of something called *The Shallow Pond and the Envelope*?"

"Sounds like something they'd name a coffeehouse in Brattleboro."

"It's a moral puzzle. A famous philosopher came up with it."

"Have I heard of him?"

I shake my head. "Doubtful."

"How do you know about the puzzle, then?"

"I read a few books, you know, when I'm not tickling the ivories. Want to give it a shot?"

Cray looks up. "Is it boring?"

"Yes, probably. But that doesn't mean you shouldn't do it."

"Fine. But if it gets really boring, I'll tell you and we'll stop."

I take a deep breath. "Okay, let's say you're driving around like we were today, and you see a young girl, a neighborhood kid, drowning in a shallow pond. What would you do?"

Cray squints. "Is this some kind of trick question?"

"No."

"I'd stop and pull her out. Just like we stopped when we saw the accident. Except everyone there was already dead, probably."

"Would you think for a moment about getting your clothes muddy?"

He shrugs. "Maybe, but I'd still wade in. It's just a shallow pond."

"Okay. So then you're back home and you get a letter from some group that wants you to give them ten dollars to keep a child from dying in the Sudan. What do you do?"

"Probably chuck it. We get about ten of those a day in Vermont. We're the bleeding heart liberal belt, you know. If they're hungry, tired, and poor, they hit us up for cash."

"But say this one's for real. And for ten dollars they really can save a child's life. Isn't that about what it might cost to get your clothes dry-cleaned?"

"Probably. So what?"

"The point is, ignoring that letter is just the same as ignoring the girl in the pond."

Cray shakes his head. "The hell it is . . . one's right in your own backyard, the other's way across the world."

I hold up my hand. "Doesn't matter. If you can help someone without much harm to yourself—just some dirty clothes, a ten-dollar bill—you ought to do it. Doesn't matter whether it's right around the corner or in another country, whether it's someone you know or a stranger."

Cray pauses for a moment, rubbing his chin slowly in his patented pose of contemplation.

I reach over and give his shoulder a gentle shove.

"Okay, okay, I agree. People ought to do whatever they can. I'm all for helping out. And as you can probably tell, I don't really give a shit about getting my clothes dirty."

"That's good, Cray."

"You know, I thought traveling around with you again was going to be boring, Uncle Ross. Hanging out in hotels, drinking a few beers, driving across the big flat states. I have to say, I tried to talk Dad out of it. But it's been a lot more interesting this time. Tons of fun. Stealing cars off the street. Stealing diamonds off naked drunk chicks. Playing after-hours clubs. Death in the afternoon. Two Amstel Lights every night. Philosophy lessons in the Waffle House. I'm learning a lot. Most of it kind of strange, by the way."

I smile. "More to come."

We drive on through the green hills of central Kentucky. Cray sleeps, exhausted. I know I should stay on the highway—it's late afternoon and we're still an hour south of Louisville. But I pull off on a county lane that runs parallel to the main road for a minute, then cuts between tobacco fields. The road twists and turns and I keep expecting to find another destroyed pickup waiting around every bend.

I pull up to a battered mailbox, reach in my fakebook, and take out $500. When I roll down the window, Cray startles.

"What're you doing?" he says.

"Giving away some money." I open the mailbox, put the cash on top of the mail, and close the door.

"To who?"

"Don't know." I roll up my window and drive on, wheels slipping in the gravel.

Cray sits up. "Where the hell are we?"

"South of Louisville."

"You just dropped a pile of cash in some stranger's mailbox, Uncle Ross, is that what you're saying?"

I nod.

Cray shakes his head. "Any particular reason why?"

"Because I can."

"So when you steal a BMW, you give all the money away?"

"I do."

"The diamonds too?"

"Yes, them too." I pull up to another mailbox, this one on Cray's side. "Mind rolling down your window?" I hand him a stack of cash.

Cray leans out the window and puts the money into the mailbox, then closes it. We drive on.

"I have to say, Uncle Ross, that doesn't seem like a great idea to me."

"Why not?"

"Probably because my duffel bag's stuffed with Dad's cash. It might as well be a stack of note cards or something that we're handing out."

"Think about it this way," I say. "You've been working in the fields since dawn, staking up the tomato plants, feeding the chickens, or whatever people around here do all day. Then you open your mailbox and find five hundred dollars in it. Wouldn't that make you feel like the world was a good place, even if you had decided that it wasn't?"

Cray thinks for a moment. "No, it wouldn't. Not really."

I lift my sunglasses and peer at my nephew, wondering why he's being so willfully dense. "What do you mean?"

"I might feel lucky or something. And it might be fun to spend the money on something I couldn't afford. But when the money was gone, I'd still feel about the same way I did before I opened the mailbox."

I stop at the next mailbox, read the painted name. "So what about Maynard Olsen here." I put the cash in the mailbox. "You're saying that if Maynard finds five hundred dollars along with the phone bill and seed catalogs—it won't make him happy?"

I pull out, leaving Maynard Olsen's mailbox in the dust.

"Sure it will," Cray says. "But it won't last very long. And when the money's gone, he'll just expect more to pop into his mailbox. Like magic. And you won't be here to give it to him. Every day he opens that mailbox he'll expect to find more. When he doesn't, he'll just be disappointed. Or messed up. You ever hear about those clowns who win the lottery and then manage to piss it all away? Nothing particularly good seems to happen when people get a pile of money for free."

I pause for a moment and wonder if I'm delivering a deadly antidote, one that promises to cure but only does more damage. "So what you're saying is that I'm handing out disappointment rather than hope?"

"That's one way of thinking about it."

"Problems instead of solutions?"

"That's another."

I jab my finger at Cray. "You're just making an excuse for doing nothing. When you're a little older, maybe you'll decide to do something to help someone else. Instead of just always thinking about yourself."

Cray holds up his hands. "Don't get all bent out of shape, Uncle Ross. It's still better than just keeping the money and buying something stupid with it like most people would."

"Glad you think so." We leave the countryside and pull back onto the main highway. Silence settles over our rental car, now a Toyota Squabble.

"I admire you, Uncle Ross, I really do," Cray says, finally. "No matter what Dad says about you, you're definitely doing something interesting, something he'd really like to know about."

"Well, I don't think it's a good idea to tell him."

"But he's your brother. Why wouldn't you tell him?"

"Lots of reasons."

"You two could collaborate," Cray says. "Yeah, that would be a GREAT THING." He pounds his fist on the dashboard and I swerve.

"What do you have in mind?"

"You could hand out Dad's cash—the whole barn's FULL OF IT!"

"I don't think giving away counterfeit twenties to people is exactly the same thing."

"So stolen money is better than fake money?"

"I didn't say that, exactly."

"But that's what you mean."

I pause. "Maybe. I'm just saying it's different. And it's not something I want to do."

"So you're a thief with morals."

"I'd like to think so."

Cray shrugs. "So do a lot of people who steal stuff."

We pass a billboard—there's a Taco Fiesta at the next exit. Cray's longing gaze stays on the billboard as we drive past it; he's missed lunch thanks to the accident.

I take the exit and pull into the crowded parking lot of Taco Fiesta. "Go," I say. "But be quick about it."

Cray jumps out of the car and walks over to my window. "Thanks, Uncle Ross!"

"Don't mention it." I'm not being nice. I'm just tired of arguing with him.

"Don't look now," Cray whispers. "But there's a BMW I-Series parked three rows away. Can I borrow the DMK?"

"You want to steal a car in broad daylight? In the middle of a parking lot?"

"Okay, so it's not such a good idea."

"Why don't you go buy a burrito instead? And pay with a fake Jackson!" Cray brightens at the thought and bounds across the parking lot.

———

The Louisville gig goes on without me. I'm sitting at the piano at the Seelbach Hilton but I'm miles away on the empty highway, looking at a crumpled pickup truck. I'm running through a set but Delmar is there, smiling at me from the front seat of his beat-up car with the shredded roof. I'm playing requests while my grandfather walks through the crowd handing out slices of watermelon.

At the end of my last set, I take a look around the Rathskeller, a medieval keep crowded with drunk tourists. My tip jar is over-flowing. They applaud and I play an encore, something they've heard before. It might as well be *Bebop Kumbaya* for all I care. I'm tired and knocked off course. I look out and see hand after hand loaded with engagement rings big as berries—oval, emerald-cut, princess, radiant, marquise, cushion-cut. But I can't muster the enthusiasm necessary to free them.

Upstairs, I turn on the light in our room and find Cray sprawled on his bed, a circle of empties around him. The TV is on—he's ordered a movie that features naked college girls show-ing off gravity-defying breast implants. It's like a catalog for Dow Corning. I click the TV off and lie down heavily on my bed. At the precise moment that my head hits the pillow, the phone rings. I pick up the receiver.

"Cray? That you?" I recognize my brother's husky voice.

"No, it's me. Cray's asleep."

"It's not even midnight."

"He had a few beers and crashed."

"I said he could have a couple of beers, max!"

"So did I," I say. "But it's been a long day. And he said you let him drink as much beer as he wants."

"Ho ho ho," Ray wheezes. "Don't you know enough not to believe a sixteen-year-old boy? He wants two things—pussy and beer. And not necessarily in that order."

"What about burritos?"

"Distant third." Ray waits, whispers, "Listen, you got to get to Washington, Ross. And fast."

"Need me to eavesdrop on the Committee of Four?"

"No, I got that covered, smart guy. And shut the fuck up about that, will you? I'm on a landline here."

"So why do I have to go to Washington?"

"Because Chief's dying."

I pause. "He's been sick before." Chief was in his mid-seventies now, with the usual litany of health problems—high blood pressure, narrowed vessels in his heart, a suspicious growth in his throat—that kept him in and out of the hospital. No ailment seemed capable of slowing the indomitable Chief.

"Well now he's really sick. Something with his esophagus, probably cancer."

"I'm playing the Hay-Adams next month. I'll stop in then."

"Not soon enough. This time we're talking weeks."

"I thought he was doing better."

"Well he's not. And if you don't go see him soon, you won't be seeing him at all. He's in Beth-Israel, oncology ICU."

I rub my eyes. "Are you going?"

"I can't just get on a plane. I'm kind of stuck here."

"That's not true. You just don't want to go because you don't like him."

Ray pauses. "I get him a little better now. It's taken me a while, but I do. Particularly now that I'm a father, I guess I can understand why Chief lost it every now and then."

"More like every day."

"And why he left us to move to D.C."

"Maybe you'll explain that at some point," I say.

"Listen, you might want to make your peace with him too, and quick like a bunny."

"Cray says that too." I envision a bunny racing maniacally to Washington in the fast lane, hopping over cars. Cray's nonstop cartoons have infected me.

"He steals all his best lines from me," Ray says. "We're all a bunch of thieves. Don't forget it."

After Ray hangs up, I call Malcolm in New York.

"I understand completely," he says after I explain why I have to go to Washington. "No worries, I can cover your next shows. Can you get back for the Netherland in Cincinnati? They're hard to please." His familiar deep voice is always comforting, no matter what he's saying.

"Definitely."

"Good. Now let me see who's available to fill in." Bar sounds filter through Malcolm's cell phone as he consults his legendary black book.

"There's a great singer out on the circuit," Malcolm tells me. "Marianne London. Caught her act?"

My heart quickens. "Just once, briefly. From a distance. She's good."

"Then maybe she's the one," Malcolm says. "She's staying in Louisville too. At the Reardon. She's got two nights there, but they don't overlap with your next gigs. When does your plane leave?"

"Eleven tomorrow morning."

"Meet her downstairs at eight. I'll set up a breakfast meeting."

"Why don't you just call her and see if she'll do the gigs?"

"Because it would be much more civilized for you to ask her yourself and work out the arrangements. Honestly, you used to be so polite."

I look over at Cray lying on his bed, sprawled in a nest of wrestling magazines, headphones, his cell phone recharger, and empty Amstel Light bottles. "I've been a little distracted lately."

"Don't let Marianne dazzle you. Or steal your heart."

"I'm not easily dazzled," I say. "Particularly at eight in the morning. And my heart is steel-belted."

"A necessary evil." He exhales smoke over the receiver. "At my age, I'm just glad my heart's still beating."

"You're healthy as a horse."

"There are many kinds of horses in all conditions," Malcolm says. "I know this from the track."

"I'm assuming that this Marianne London is just a singer."

A pause. "I believe she plays some piano as well."

"And?"

"And she's elegant and thoroughly charming. That's all I can tell you." Malcolm clicks his phone off.

At eight-thirty, I sit waiting in the cheery hotel restaurant with families on vacation, a couple of businessmen reading the *Courier-Journal,* but no singers, charming or otherwise.

The waitress gives me a knowing glance as she refills my water glass for the third time. Being stood up for breakfast is pathetic. I notice her rings are cheap.

Fifteen minutes later, as I stand up to go back to the room, the waitress screams, then a plate shatters. A dog barks. An older woman shouts "Chloe! Chloe!" over and over and reaches down to retrieve what appears to be a dog about the size of a ferret. I wonder when people were allowed to bring dogs to breakfast. I think of the scraped dog by the side of the road.

"I hate dogs, too," a low voice mutters.

I look over to find Marianne London in a black silk blouse sitting across from me. "I didn't see you walk in, sorry." I reach over and shake her hand. "Ross. Ross Wolfshead."

She squints.

"Ross Clifton. That's my stage name, you know, the one Malcolm gave me." My eyes are drawn to her elegant diamond necklace, three discreet marquis stones along a nearly invisible gold chain.

She nods. "I thought so. I'm Marianne London, formerly Mary Rose Williams of Jacksonville, Florida. Malcolm told me about your father. I'm very sorry. My mother's been really sick for a long time, and I know how hard it can be, believe me."

"Thanks," I say.

The waitress walks over and Marianne orders a cup of black coffee and steak and eggs. I try not to cringe.

"I hear you're the best piano player on the circuit. And Malcolm's met a lot of them."

"Nice of him to say that," I say. "I caught part of your set once. In St. Louis. At the . . ."

"Ambassador Hotel," she says. "Great night. I spotted you sitting in the audience like some kind of jazz spy. Gave you my version of a table dance and you still cut out early. So are you shy or rude?" She smiles.

"Both. Neither."

"Well, we'll have to figure that out at some point. For now, I'll assume shy."

"Thank you—and thanks for picking up my next few shows," I say, the last words I speak for almost an hour. I hand her the list and she puts it in the pocket of her dress without looking at it, then takes a deep breath. Her eyes close for a moment as if in prayer.

The words emerge slowly at first, then with increasing numbers of asides, clauses, jokes, interludes, reminiscences, thoughts, counterthoughts, and even brief snatches of song. Her thoughts are like exotic invasives nudging out the tiresome rows of garden-variety conversation.

During the onslaught of words, Marianne pulls at her long hair, graceful fingers twisting the streaked reddish strands. She holds her narrow chin, runs a finger along her graceful eyebrow. She reminds me of a very smart schoolgirl who has been called upon unexpectedly to answer a teacher's question, then finds it impossible to stop.

Somehow, during her monologue, she manages to eat her breakfast so gracefully that I forget to be disgusted by the sight of red meat before noon.

I find myself looking at Marianne, really looking at her, and not just at her jewelry. She reminds me of a taller, less speckled Julianne Moore. High cheekbones, a graceful neck, straight shoulders—it all adds up to confident and elegant. And excellent posture, my mother would have pointed out. Her eyes, intense and green, sweep the room at the end of every sentence as if she's looking for something.

As Marianne speaks volumes, I glance at my watch, find that my flight is in less than an hour. A lot less. I have heard about Marianne's childhood in Florida, singing in her mother's road-house. My father is dying in Washington, D.C., but Marianne is pushing any tragedy into the middle distance with her voice.

Every song she mentions turns out to be one of my favorites. Each incident she recounts resonates with my own collection of road stories. I am enthralled. And about to miss my plane.

She grabs my hand. "I'm so sorry, I've lost all track of time. Let me drive you to the airport."

"That would be great." I leave some bills on the table, wondering if they include any of my brother's handiwork. Cray has been seeding my wallet with Jacksons lately. Then I grab my bag and follow Marianne through the restaurant, barely able to keep up.

Out on the street, Marianne strides to a steel-gray Mercedes sedan with tinted glass, straightens her pleated skirt beneath her knees as she climbs in.

"Fine car," I say. "The circuit must be treating you well."

Marianne gives me a flat look. "Malcolm's been keeping me booked. But the car's a present from an admirer. They're always giving me things I can't afford. If you have to sing for your supper, you end up eating a lot of lentils. You know that."

I get in the car. "I like lentils."

"I do too, just not every day."

"So you rely on gifts from kindhearted strangers?"

"Some aren't so kindhearted. And some aren't strangers." Marianne pulls onto the highway, driving in the French manner, heedless and fast, trusting fate. "I just take what they give me as a kind of windfall."

"Don't they expect something in return?" I'm fishing for her angle.

Marianne frowns. "Some do. But they don't get it. These are gentlemen. And I'm no pushover, Ross."

I consider the differences in our semi-parallel careers. Marianne's uptown admirers give her expensive gifts. Women unwittingly donate their diamonds to me. My nightwork seems so crass, mercantile, and hands-on compared with her elegant world of gentlemen and champagne.

Marianne downshifts and takes the airport exit. The car is quiet for a moment, sealed off from the strip malls, car lots, and carpet warehouses racing by. I settle into the seat and smell Marianne—some kind of lavender skin lotion and smokiness blending in with the car's leather and teak interior. I see her delicate fingers wrapped casually around the steering wheel, see gold glimmering on the ring finger of her right hand. I gaze coldly at the glittering diamond in the center, cut in the old-fashioned asscher style, flanked by two emeralds.

"Three carats," she says without turning toward me. "From an admirer in Texas. It was his wife's."

"What happened to her?"

"She got old."

I nod.

"Worried about your father?"

"Guess so," I say. The Chief in my mind is vibrant and powerful, a sharp, fast roll on a rattling snare. I am less sure about who waits for me.

"My mother's in a memory-loss ward in Hollywood, Florida," Marianne says softly. "Started forgetting little things a few years back, sending me birthday cards over and over. She got worse really quickly. Now she has no idea who I am."

"I'm really sorry. That's terrible."

"Her insurance only covers part of it. I pay about seventy thousand dollars a year to keep her alive, though you can hardly call it living. I can't even think of her as my mother anymore. I loved my mother—she ran a bar back in Florida, had hundreds of stories. I guess I learned to talk too much from her. But now she's like a blank slate. Doesn't talk hardly at all. Watches airplanes."

I say nothing.

"So all the admirers really do come in handy. And not just for me." She turns and smiles at me. Her sunglasses are dark, but I detect a glistening at the corners of her eyes.

"I understand. I really do," I say. Marianne relies on gifts; I rely on stealing. She gives her money to her mother; I give mine to strangers.

"We're here." She takes off her sunglasses, reveals green eyes flecked with deep yellow.

"Thanks for the ride—and for covering for me. I owe you." In our short time together, I've become an ardent admirer. "Oh, I almost forgot one thing."

"What's that?"

"My nephew, Cray. He's sixteen. He's traveling with me, kind of like summer school, I guess. Can you give him a ride to Cincinnati?"

"Is he as nice as you are?"

"Nice, no. Interesting, yes."

"I'd welcome the company. I get tired of driving alone. It'll be nice to have someone along for the ride, someone to talk to."

You have no idea, I think. "That's incredibly helpful. I'll have him meet you in the lobby at noon."

She shakes her head. "Glad to do it. When are you coming back?"

"In a few days. Playing the Netherland, then doing some gigs out East."

Marianne smiles. "So am I. We've been playing the same towns for months, just a couple of days before or after. Funny, isn't it?"

"Yes, funny." I'm glad she's been noticing me. Our schedules are almost synchronized, as if Malcolm has planned it. And maybe he has.

"It's almost like we were supposed to meet, eventually."
Marianne reaches over—to open the door, I assume—but instead, she rests her warm hand gently on my knee, leans toward
me, and presses her soft lips against mine for a moment, then
pulls back. *A kiss to build a dream on,* as the song goes.

I stare at her, stunned. Usually I'm the one delivering first-
strike affection.

"Your plane could blow up. I could wreck my car on the way
back to the hotel," she says. "Life's way too short to wait for all
the lights to turn green, Ross."

"I'll remember that."

She smiles. "I hope you will."

I shoulder my bag and climb awkwardly out of her car. I lean
down and tap on the window. Some nascent thought is rising up
in my mind and urging me to blurt it out. I have only a glimmer
of this unformed notion, know only that it's about us and attrac-
tion and fate. I'm sure I'll come up with something to say, ide-
ally something that charms and intrigues this beautiful, familiar
stranger. But Marianne pulls out abruptly, leaving me standing
on the curb with the cabdrivers and tourists.

washington, d.c.

Chief quit Moore's Frozen Foods after twenty years, certain it was about to be bought out by the dreaded Birds Eye. He took a job in Washington, heading up the American Labor Council, an organization Reagan created to undermine American labor. Chief didn't see any irony in working for an organization named after its intended target. His big payoff had come along. An anticlimactic, late-night departure to Washington ended our family, such that it was.

I was eighteen, in my first year at the University of Chicago.

Ray lived on the southside and played drums in a punk band called Filthy Lucre. Our mother, Eileen, stayed in our Lake Forest dream home, now creepily quiet. At first, she was happy to be free of Chief's powerful orbit. A few months later, she was diagnosed with leukemia. She died within a year, about the time their divorce became final. Chief always made much of the timing, as if her unwillingness to follow him to Washington caused her disease and death.

"If only she had come with me," he would say, not remembering that she wasn't invited. No one was. Chief always worked solo.

Somewhere over West Virginia I look down at the patchwork of green fields and tiny veins of highway and suddenly wish that Ray was with me, or Marianne, or even Cray. I'm alone and silent on the underbooked flight to Dulles, just me and the financial services, pharmaceutical, and software guys with their laptops and business banter.

Chief is in the Transition and Recovery Center section of the ICU. Along the ward, gray-faced people sit in bed, watching televisions mounted to the ceiling. Voices, alarms, phones, announcements over an intercom—the hospital sounds as dissonant as a youth orchestra. Except every patient is old and half-dead.

The door is open a crack. I wait outside Chief's crowded room for a moment and eavesdrop. Chief sits in a chair, issuing opinions about various stocks to a clump of strangers. His second wife, Vivian, knits quietly in the corner.

Chief met Vivian seven years ago on a cruise ship and married her a few months later. They knew each other from Washington, where she was a tobacco lobbyist. I know little about their life together except that they have a town house in Bethesda and they travel a lot.

I knock. The conversation stops.

"Come in," Vivian shouts.

Chief sits in a brown leatherette hospital chair, semi-reclined, as if awaiting the arrival of a dentist. He raises his head slightly, sees me, then smiles and waves me over.

"Ross! I thought you'd never get here. You're not easy to find, you know."

"Hello, Dad." I walk over to his chair and Chief stretches a splotchy hand from beneath the white blanket. Tubes are taped to his wrist and run up to an IV rack. Larger tubes run from his throat to a blue box on the floor. Wires sprout from his big toe, its nail yellowed as an old domino.

"Ladies and gentlemen, just in from tickling the ivories throughout the United States, my son Ross." He pats my back gently for a moment, then puts his hand back beneath the blanket. We're together again, father and son, Chief and thief.

I stand awkwardly in front of three strangers about my own age.

Vivian puts her knitting in a beach bag and gives me a hug. "Very nice of you to come all this way," she says, then leans forward and whispers, "He's better today, Ross. But he's really not doing well."

I nod.

"You've met my boys, haven't you?" Vivian waves a dismissive hand at the trio.

"I don't think so."

I shake hands with Jim, Rick, and Frankie. One wears a shiny blue jogging outfit, another is in a brown suit, and the third is in a sports jersey and jeans. They are all twice my size and rise from their chairs only with a great deal of grunting. Once up, my stepbrothers huddle for a moment and decide to take a break from sitting around the room to go sit in the hospital cafeteria. These interlopers are my family, in a sense, but I'm glad to see them go.

"Dressed like a damn waiter . . ." I hear one say as they lumber down the hall.

"They're good boys," Vivian says. "All in real estate."

I nod. Had we met when we actually were boys, we might have been friends, but it seems unlikely. They wouldn't have met the Wolfshead standard of deviousness. Ray would have shaken them down for every cent they had.

"I'm sure you two will want to get caught up," Vivian says, picking up her knitting bag and rising to follow her sons.

Suddenly, I am alone with my father. Chief sits in the lounge chair, with his tubes coming from everywhere, surrounded by a bank of electronics that reminds me inappropriately of Rick Wakeman, a keyboard player Ray used to blast in junior high school to torment me.

Chief points to the television. "Turn that shit off, will you?"

I pick up the remote and click it.

He struggles to press a button on the side of his chair, then finds the right one and closes his eyes briefly.

"They let me control the pain medication," he says. "All I do is punch this button and I feel better. I used to punch it every hour or so. Now I'm lucky to get more than five minutes out of every punch. I'm high as a neighborhood of junkies."

I nod.

His gleaming eyes zero in on me. "I'm dying. Ray told you that, didn't he?"

I say nothing, look away.

"Well, it's true. I'm done with all the heroics. There's some operation where they replace the esophagus with a piece of my colon—no comments, please—but they evaluated me and decided it would kill me. Anyway, I'm seventy-eight. That's about as long as the warranty lasts. After that, it's overtime."

The Chief I see in front of me, yellow skin crosshatched as old leather, hands waxen on the hospital blanket, eyes shiny, fails to match up with the mythical father I carry with me in my memory.

"You never were much of a talker." Chief lays his hand gently over mine, a tender gesture I can't remember him ever doing before. "Always upstairs with your coins."

I was the one downstairs pounding away on the spinet, but I don't bother pointing this out. This is not the time for corrections.

"I've been wanting to ask you something." Chief bends closer, wincing for a moment, then pressing the painkiller button. "For a long time now. But we don't see you in Washington much."

"I don't play D.C. very often," I lie. I've played D.C. every three months or so for years. I just never bothered to tell Chief and Vivian about my gigs at the Hay-Adams—and they never seemed that interested.

"I'd really like to see you play," he says. "A little late for that now. But I'm sure you're very good. You always practiced so much. I never even had to ask you to, not like Ray and his drums."

"It's not a bad way to make a living." At first I never invited Chief to any gigs because Ray and I were still furious at him. Later, I thought Chief would find it demeaning to see his son tickling the ivories in front of mid-level bureaucrats, lobbyists, and drunken lawyers. After all, Chief shook the hands of three presidents, did a couple of star turns in front of grand juries.

"It's more than that, son," he says. "You're doing what you want. Just like me, just like your grandfather. He wanted to do nothing but grow watermelons. And that's what he did every day until he died. He was also seventy-eight when he died, by the way. You may want to make note of that. Seems to be the family checkout time."

"Got it."

A nurse—red-haired and smiling—comes in, looks at various tubes, connections, relays, reservoirs. She's charmed by Chief; it's clear that he's well-known to the nurses.

They chat while the nurse takes his blood pressure, then she scrawls notes on the clipboard at the end of the bed.

I wander over to the wall of cards, find several signed by senators. I flip open a big Hallmark card with a photo of tulips on it—HOPE YOU'RE FEELING BETTER! Inside, it's signed by James D. Croton. Ray's nemesis on the Committee of Four is Chief's crony—all the connections start to click together.

I raise my eyebrows, then untape the card from the wall and slip it into my pocket for Ray. I drift back over to the bedside.

"She's in a messy divorce," Chief whispers after the nurse is gone. "Litigation, restraining orders, the whole nine yards. I hooked her up with a mediator friend of mine. Maybe they can work it out without giving all their money to lawyers. Seems kind of hopeless, though. She's angry. That never gets you anywhere." He shrugs. "Negotiating contracts with the toughest union bastards is a lot simpler than negotiating love." A wry smile, a wave of his hand.

"Nice of you to help out."

"You do what you can," he says. "I'd like to think it improves matters, but now I'm not so sure you really can help anyone else. What's going to happen is just going to happen. It's like trying to fight gravity. I tried to help out the unions when I was with Moore's. There are those who said otherwise, but I really did try to get them a fair shake, one that they wouldn't have to renegotiate every year. And all I got for it was a lot of static from the higher-ups and the lower-downs, too." He shakes his head. "Remember when the union guys used to call up and yell on the phone?"

I nod.

"And they shot our little dog once—what was his name?"

"Windy," I say, a little too quickly.

He nods. "And they tried to burn our house down back when we lived in Lake Forest. And I suppose this helped split your mother and me apart, break up the team." Another history-dispelling wave of his ancient hand. "Back to what I was saying earlier . . ."

"About what?"

"About having to tell you something. I'll be quick about it. At this point I have to be quick about everything." He looks directly into my eyes. "I'm sorry about how things went, Ross, you know, back in Chicago. I really am. I know that my job took up most of my time. But that was the way it was back then."

I nod.

"And I know that the divorce from . . ."

"Eileen?" I say.

"Of course, Eileen, your mother. It's the painkillers. I know that was terrible, too. But again, that's just the way things went back in the Reagan era. You flexed your power and didn't think about the consequences. You got divorced and did your own thing." Chief pauses for a moment, struggles to catch his breath.

"And I had to come to Washington. I really didn't have a choice. The offer was just too good. It was a dream come true."

This is my cue in the ancient ballad of father and son. "I understand," I say. "That was a long time ago."

Chief nods. "I'd tell Ray, but I can't seem to get him on an airplane. Maybe he's too fat by now."

I laugh. "He just doesn't like to travel."

"Says his work really keeps him busy—what's he doing these days?"

"He's a . . . printer. He does high-end jobs, really beautiful work." I'm not sure how much Chief knows.

"Seems like even a fancy printer could take a couple of days off to visit his father. Particularly given my current condition."

I nod, leave it to Ray to explain himself.

"He's not really a printer, you know," Chief says quietly. "He's doing something for the government. Something very secret. That's what he told me."

"That's what he told you?" In a way, it's true, Ray is doing government work, though James D. Croton and the Bureau of Engraving might not agree.

"Yeah, national security stuff. He's helping his country. Printing in inks that no one can detect. Microscopic messages. Things of that sort. He always had a scientific . . ." Chief's chin drifts down and his eyes close. The red lights on one of the monitors blink more slowly, then click off. He slumps to one side in his chair and starts to struggle to breathe, making a terrible wheezing sound. An alarm bleats and a red emergency light over the door flashes.

A few seconds later, nurses, doctors, interns, and Vivian rush in, followed by her three sons, who glare at me. The doctors ease Chief down to the floor and cut off his pajamas. I stand at the back of the room, helpless, watching the medical team strug-gling to restart my father's heart. *He's Bradying down,* someone shouts. I have no idea what that means, though it doesn't sound good. An Indian doctor in an immaculate turban gives him an injection in his thigh. The doctors prepare to apply bright orange electrical paddles to the caved chest of my father's yellow twin.

It can't possibly be Chief on the floor, withered and spotted with moles, muscles turned to loose flesh clinging to narrow bone. The powerful father I carry with me in memory and the dying man I see lying so still on the floor become one. My father is dying right in front of me. Inconceivable as it seems, my in-vincible father, the ultimate solo artist, is dying.

The alarm bells stop and the doctors pause. The Indian doc-tor shrugs. Chief opens his eyes, heavy-lidded and unfocused, and looks directly at me.

The doctors lift Chief back into his chair, examine him, wave a flashlight in his eyes, listen to his heart. But the urgency has passed and relief settles over the room, fear dissipating as the interns and my stepbrothers drift out of the room.

"This has been happening a lot lately," Vivian tells me, dry-ing her eyes with a balled-up tissue. "Something about his heart rhythm going haywire. Not a good sign."

I nod. The truth is that Chief is too tough to die. He's man-aged to negotiate himself a little more time.

When the crowd leaves, I sit quietly in the room for a mo-ment, watch the sunlight on the floor.

After a few minutes, Chief stirs, waves his fingers at me, beckoning me toward him. "We weren't finished," he says softly. "Before my heart stopped and we were so rudely interrupted, I had something . . ." He pauses, catches his breath. "To tell you. Something important."

I lean forward, ready for the dark family secret, the affair, the brother or sister I never knew about.

"They may tell you . . ."

"Yes."

"People may tell you that negotiating is about getting your way, about how much you can take from someone," he says clearly, resolutely. "But that's not right. It's about . . . how much they're willing to give up." He smiles. "Remember this. I think it's important. I know you probably don't. But please remember it."

Chief's head tilts back on the pillow and he slips into sleep, exhausted. Vivian shakes her head, sits back in her chair, takes out her knitting.

I say goodbye to Vivian, promise to come back tomorrow morning. In the brief time I've spent with her over the years, I've come to appreciate her as a kind woman who has given up plenty to take care of Chief.

Guilt catches up with me in the parking lot. I've been a bad son, refusing to stay in touch with my father. Instead, I've been hiding out on the road. And worse: I've forgotten how to be with people who aren't strangers in an audience.

Sickness and anxiety hover over the hospital parking lot. Some of the cars in the lot belong to new parents, to the cured, repaired, those in remission. But not many. Most belong to people who are here waiting for someone to die. I reach into my fakebook and take out a stack of fifties. I put one under every windshield wiper as I walk down a row that stretches off into the distance.

"Hey!"

I turn around. A security guard in a blue blazer cuts between two cars.

"You can't put nothing on the cars. It's against the rules." He points to a sign at the edge of the lot. "No soliciting."

I say nothing, just wander toward the end of the lot, where the city streets begin.

The guard plucks the bill from the windshield and stares at it, confused. "Hey!"

I run, fakebook tucked under my arm.

I only have about thirty yards on the guard, a college running back, apparently. He barrels across the parking lot and follows me down the street, crowded at the end of the workday. A bus stops and lets out its passengers directly in front of me. I dodge around the crowd. In a few moments, the guard will shout and they'll have me on the ground.

I toss the stack of bills in the air. The crowd pauses for a moment, turning silent as they take in the fluttering rain of cash, trying to figure out if it's real.

Then, complete chaos.

The crowd descends on the money like locusts on leaves. An old woman falls on the ground, clutching a handful of bills and howling. A kid in a baseball hat grabs a twenty out of her hands. I walk quickly toward my hotel, head down.

When the phone rings, I'm lying sprawled on the bed, still wearing my suit.

"I'm getting ready to do your gig, any advice?"

"Don't sing *Moondance*."

"Never in a million years." Marianne pauses. "I wish you were here, Ross."

"I do too, believe me." I tell Marianne about Chief, details I haven't thought of in years. The stories flood out of me as if I'm talking in my sleep.

"It may not be over all neat and tidy, you know," she says. "My mother's been hanging on for years and they told me she'd be dead a long time ago. That's part of the wonders of modern medicine. You can stick around until there's almost nothing left."

I think of Chief and his jump-started heart. "There's probably plenty of fight in him still. He's pretty tough."

"Like his son."

"No, not at all like his son."

"Don't be so sure. You don't spend fifteen years on the hotel circuit without growing a thick skin."

I think of Marianne's skin.

"You're quiet," she says.

"Just thinking."

"About what?"

I pause. "About you."

"Keep thinking about me for a while. At least until my second set's over. Might bring me luck, or at least keep the creeps away. You probably never had a drunken CEO reach down your dress, did you?"

"Can't say that I have."

"Well, it isn't pretty."

"Have Cray serve as your personal bouncer."

"He's gone. Haven't seen him since we got here."

I wonder what this news means.

"He's a good driver, by the way. Seemed to really like my car. But he didn't say much, just asked if I wouldn't mind a quick stop at a—"

"Cheap disgusting Mexican restaurant."

"How did you know?"

"Believe me, I know. And he ordered . . . let me guess . . . a burrito."

"You're right again. Then after we got to Cincinnati, we sat in the bar for a little while, downstairs. It's a nice one, very Art Deco. He had—"

"A pile of Amstel Lights."

"You're psychic."

"Just a little too familiar with my nephew. I have to say, I kind of miss the little freak."

"When you come back, we'll have a party."

"All of us?"

"No, just you and me."

"And just what do you mean by that?"

At this point, our conversation lapses into the low and pause-filled dialect of desire. I fall asleep to the sound of Marianne talking, so soothing and far away.

The sound of my complimentary newspaper being shoved under the door wakes me. I stand, wavering for a moment, wonder where I am.

Though I drank nothing last night, I feel hungover. I said too much to Marianne and our hours of conversation have left me raw and exhausted.

Wandering around the hotel room, I play a melody in the air with my right hand, a Jack Teagarden number. I miss playing the piano. I miss driving to the next gig, watching the city lights shimmer at night. I miss Marianne. I even miss Cray, though not that much.

The phone rings.

"Good morning, beautiful," I say.

"Ross, it's me, Vivian." My stepmother sounds confused for a moment.

"Oh, sorry. I was—" My mind goes blank. "I was expecting a call from someone else."

"Well, I won't keep you long. I just wanted to thank you for coming by yesterday. Your father was really glad to see you."

"How's he feeling?"

"He had a hard night. Lots of pain. He's still sleeping."

"I'm sorry." I hear voices in the background.

"I'm calling with a quick question, Ross. Do you have a copy of this morning's paper?"

I look over at the door to my room, see the *Washington Post* waiting on the carpet. "I do."

"Turn to the Metro section."

I do as I'm told, read the headline—MAN TOSSES CASH TO CROWD, FIVE ARRESTED. My stomach sinks.

"Do you see that photo at the bottom?"

"Yes." The blurry photo from a camera phone shows people on their knees, scrambling for cash on the sidewalk. Far in the background, I see myself walking away, my black suit coat flailing in the wind. Even in the distance, I look like a crazy person fleeing the scene of the crime. I shake my head, sense Miles by my side, rolling his milky eyes, saying, *You are one stupid white motherfucker.*

"My sons think the guy in the background, the one who caused all the trouble, looks like you."

I read the article, find out that police are searching for an unnamed man who caused a brief riot at a bus stop. "I'm looking at the photo now, Vivian, and I can see why they might say that, but it's not me. I took a cab back to the hotel right after I saw you."

"The security guard came around asking everyone questions. Rick told him he remembered that you were wearing a black suit. He said you looked like a waiter or an undertaker, no offense."

I freeze for a moment. "None taken, Vivian. Just let Rick know that the guy in the photo couldn't possibly be me. I was pretty upset after seeing Dad and just wanted to get back to the hotel. Besides, I don't make enough money to do something like that."

"That's what Rick and the other boys decided," Vivian says. "They said a musician like you wouldn't be throwing money around. They figured it must be a drug dealer or someone like that. Someone who had tons of cash."

"Exactly."

"Well, just thought I'd check. Have a good flight back."

"Thanks, tell Dad I . . . I'll see him soon."

"I will."

The phone clicks and Vivian is gone. I drop the phone and stare at the photograph again, searching for the grace, the goodness along the sidewalk. I cringe. It looks like a piñata of cash has just burst. The people who ended up with the money probably weren't poor. They were just greedy, and the world already rewards them without any help from me.

I toss the paper across the room and it breaks into sheets that flutter in the morning air, then settle on the carpet, a thin gray layer of bad news.

cincinnati

Cray sprints through our hotel room at the Westin like a happy cartoon dog whose owner has returned after a long weekend away. He's taking my bag, pouring me a bowl of brown rice chips he bought at a health food store, cleaning the skyline of Amstel Light bottles from the bedside table—all pretty much simultaneously.

"You okay, nephew?"

"Yeah, yeah, never better." Cray's head bobs up and down.

"Kind of late to be drinking coffee." My flight was delayed

for a couple of hours because of fog. By the time I got a cab over the river to Cincinnati, it was after midnight.

"Didn't have any all day. Been too busy, way too busy."

"Doing what?"

Cray smiles, walks to the window, and puts one trembling hand on the plastic-tipped string that opens the blinds. "Remember how you told me to do something to help other people?"

"Yeah, kind of."

Cray's panting. "Ready?"

"I'm ready."

"Close your eyes."

"Okay. They're closed."

"No they're not," Cray says. "You're peeking."

"Now they're really closed, I promise." I open my eyes when I hear the click of the blinds. Several floors below us, I see the hotel parking lot, exactly the same as the hundreds of others I've looked out at over the years.

"Very funny." I'm starting to grasp Cray's elaborate sense of irony.

He grabs my arm. "Uncle Ross, look a little closer."

I squint down at the parking lot, lit by tall vapor lights that glow in the foggy night.

"And then . . ." I roll my hand in front of me, waiting for the secret.

Cray squares my shoulders and points my gaze down at the parking lot. "A clue. Ultimate. Driving. Machine."

I look again and notice that almost every car in the rows beneath our windows is a BMW—sports coupes, 5-Series sedans, a few Z4s, an M3 convertible, even an old Bavaria. "Tell me this is a coincidence."

Cray smiles, shakes his head, holds up the Dealer Master Key, which I'd left hidden in the back of the nightstand drawer.

I push Cray against the wall and speak directly into his face. "Do you know what you've done? What this means?"

"You'll have lots of money to give away to people who need it?"

"It means we're in trouble, Cray. That's what it means. You steal that many BMWs and the cops definitely notice. This is not a particularly big city. That's why I always steal one BMW at a time. I'm not greedy, Cray. I don't try to clear the entire downtown of BMWs like . . . like some kind of crazed used-car salesman. This isn't a game. It isn't BMW Slayer!" I turn away and pace the room.

A pause. "I thought you'd be happy, Uncle Ross."

"No, Cray. I'm not happy. I'm worried. Very worried. Worried that all those burritos and Amstel Lights and energy drinks have created some sort of imbalance in your brain. That maybe you're incapable of rational thought."

Cray shrugs, walks to the minibar. "That's a little harsh, don't you think?"

"Harsh! Harsh? Harsh is the ten-year sentence for grand theft auto. By the time you get out, your girlfriend back in Vermont will be married and pregnant with her third child. By the time you get out, there won't be hard currency anymore and your father will be out of a job. By the time you get out, I'll be playing *Moondance* in a Motel 6 bar."

Cray's brow wrinkles. "I don't think they have a bar in a Motel 6. Just a coffeemaker and a TV, maybe some free doughnuts if you're lucky."

I kneel on the floor and press my forehead into the carpet. "Help me, somebody. Help me."

"I'll help you," Cray says softly.

I look up. "You'll help me? You? You stole my Dealer Master Key and went on a car-theft bender."

"I think the word *stole* is kind of relative in this case, Uncle Ross. I mean, you can't steal something that's already stolen. And that you use to steal other things."

"Yes you can."

"No you can't."

"Yes you can."

"No you can't."

"Shut up!"

Cray gives me his hurt puppy look. He pops the top off an Amstel Light and drains it in a couple of pulls.

"Great, now you're going to be stupid *and* drunk."

"I don't think you're being very cool, Uncle Ross. It's not really my fault."

"Then whose fault is it?"

"I tried to hang at the bar with your girl Marianne, but she was with some very rich gentlemen. You might want to ask her about that. One gave me a twenty and told me to get lost. Kind of a stupid expression. I mean, with GPS, you can't get lost anymore."

"So what'd you do?"

"I put it with my stack of twenties. He was impressed."

"Sorry I missed that."

"After that, I got tired of eating chili and walking around the skyways or whatever they're called, these sidewalks that go between department stores. So I decided to surprise you and take your mind off Grandpa being sick and all. Not to mention that your girlfriend is hanging out with some very rich-looking dudes."

"That's none of your business."

"Apparently it *is* her business. Men, that is."

Though I know they are just admirers, a wave of jealousy cycles through me. "She's not my girlfriend, in case you didn't notice. I just met her."

"She's got some pretty major diamonds. Maybe you should steal them."

"Thanks for that advice. Here's some from me. Don't steal a dozen BMWs, dumbass."

"Actually, I stole eighteen," he says.

I stand and pluck the DMK from Cray's hand. "Grab your jacket."

"Where we going?"

"To return some cars."

"What kind of thief steals stuff and then returns it?"

"One that doesn't want to get caught."

"That doesn't sound like any fun at all." Cray pouts.

"More fun than prison? Where they probably never have burritos, and definitely no beer?"

Cray pauses for a moment. "Yes, more fun than prison where there are probably never burritos and definitely no beer, Uncle Ross," he recites back at me in a monotone.

We take the elevator down to the lobby in icy silence.

Out in the parking lot, I stare at the BMWs. I know where the processor has his shop, but he won't take more than a couple of cars.

"Do you remember where you found them?"

"You mean exactly where I found every car, Uncle Ross?"

"Yes."

Cray shakes his head. "No way."

"What street they were on?"

He shrugs. "Kind of. All the streets are in a grid downtown. They're either numbered or named after trees."

"Okay, let's start with this one." I point the DMK at a 7-Series sedan, silver, a year or two old. The doors click open and we get in. The car smells of cigarettes and aftershave. I pull on a pair of leather driving gloves. No fingerprints tonight. I toss another pair to Cray.

"I found it a couple of streets over, I think," Cray says. "Just take a left out of the lot and I'll get you there."

We drive through the empty downtown streets, a low fog smearing the streetlights and making our whole operation seem even more shady.

"Here!" Cray points. "Close enough." I park the car next to a meter.

We get out and I lock the doors behind us, leaving the car for its puzzled owner to find in the morning.

"This is going to take forever," I say as we run back toward the parking lot. Ahead, I see a patch of the thick, dark Ohio River and the lights of northern Kentucky burning hazily in the distance. "And downtown is deserted. What are we going to say if we get stopped?"

"That we're musicians out for a walk?"

"Try again, they always think musicians have drugs."

"We're car thieves who were seized by a sudden bout of guilt?" Cray says.

"Too honest."

"We're insomniacs, and driving other people's cars is the only thing that helps?"

We stop near the post office. "Sure, Cray. I'm sure the Cincinnati police would be very sensitive to our sleep disorders.

Perhaps they'd even give us a ride in their squad car until we started to feel a little bit sleepy."

"No need to be mean, Uncle Ross, geez." Cray shakes his head.

We ferry a handful of the cars downtown, each one farther afield. Cray had days to round up his BMW collection. Now we're trying to disperse it in a few hours. Returning cars is much harder and slower than stealing them. My anger at Cray multiplies as I stalk down the streets, shirt soaked in sweat, hair hanging in tangled strands.

We deliver Car Six, a red M3 with a vanity plate that says TOP-GUN, which makes me want to push the tacky convertible into the river. Instead, we leave it up on Vine Street, then begin the long walk back to our hotel.

We rest for a moment in the parking lot. I look at my watch. "We've been doing this for about two hours and we still have twelve more cars to go. It's going to be morning by the time we're done."

Cray says nothing, puts his silver headphones on.

I look at an old Bavaria, white and battered, held together with duct tape, worthless to the Chinese, who only want the latest models. "How'd you steal this one? It doesn't even have power doors."

Cray shrugs, pulls off his headphones. "It was unlocked and I found the keys over the visor."

"Someone was mighty trusting."

"Never again."

I grab Cray by the shoulders. "Do you have the keys?"

Cray reaches into his jacket pocket, holds them up.

"Okay, here's the plan. I can follow you in the Bavaria and drive you back to the lot."

"Like a carpool," Cray says brightly. "We'll be reducing our carbon footprint, too."

I stare at him. "This really isn't a game, Cray. We have to get these cars back before morning."

Cray gets in Car Seven, a dark blue Z4. I follow him, staying a couple of blocks behind to avoid looking like a BMW parade. He drops the car on Walnut Street and I pick him up. He rocks back and forth as we drive back to the hotel, rubbing the thighs of his cargo pants with his palms.

"There's Amstel Light at the end of the tunnel, Cray."

Cray nods. "That was a good one, Uncle Ross. A *bon mot*."

"Glad you appreciate it. It's my job to keep you entertained."

"I want to go back to Vermont," he says suddenly.

"That's fine, Cray," I snap. "Tomorrow morning, you'll be on the bus." Cray's time with me hasn't exactly helped him find his way. And now it's over.

We're both silent as our battered commuter car lurches through downtown, past bars and restaurants, stores and news-stands, all closed and dark.

Cray stares at something, then reaches toward the ashtray. He holds up a wrinkled plastic bag. "Now I know why this guy left his car unlocked. He was way high and forgot." Cray tucks the bag into his pocket.

"Put that back."

Cray cringes. "Get real, Uncle Ross. We steal this stoner's car, use it to drive all over downtown all night, but you won't let me take his sad little bag of weed?"

"No, put it back."

Cray takes out a stack of twenties, peels off a few, and puts them where the bag used to be. "There, I'll pay for it."

"With money your dad printed."

Cray shakes his head. "What's the difference, Uncle Ross? What's the big diff?"

I know that there is a difference, and that it's important. But it's late and my thoughts are as hazy as the steaming night air.

Cray returns the last car, a black 5-Series sedan that looks new. I lurk back a few blocks in the battered Bavaria with squeaking suspension and tape holding the passenger door and trunk closed. I pass Fountain Square, where a peaceful bronze figure of a woman at the top of the fountain sprays water from her hands in an aquatic stigmata.

A police car swoops out of an underground parking garage, lights flashing, and pulls directly behind Cray.

"Shit." I slam my hand on the steering wheel and pull into the shadows near a bank.

A policeman climbs out of the squad car, walks over to Cray, and shines a flashlight in his eyes. I roll down my window but I can't hear what they're saying. In a moment, the policeman takes a step back and Cray climbs out of the car, hands in the air.

"*Shit!*"

The cop signals him to lower his hands, then throws him face-first against the patrol car. I see the flash of handcuffs behind Cray's back. Before the cop can fasten them, Cray turns and his lips move, a bad sign.

"Shut up, Cray," I whisper.

The policeman pulls out his nightclub and shoves one end into Cray's stomach. He crumples.

The cop kicks Cray over and over. I knock the Bavaria in gear and press the gas pedal down, driving toward the policeman as fast as I can. He takes a step back and struggles to get his pistol out of its holster. Cray is curled up on the ground, his screams cutting through the roar of the Bavaria's untuned engine.

The policeman is in my headlights. He turns slightly toward me and I see his pale, fleshy face, eyes reflecting like a deer's.

I press the brake pedal down as hard as I can. The tires screech. The car skids then jerks to a stop and the tape on the passenger's door gives way. The door swings open and slams into the cop, sends him flying through the air.

The street is quiet. All I hear is my heart pounding.

I get out carefully and walk toward the cop, lying motionless on the asphalt. I reach down and put my hand on his neck. He's unconscious but alive.

"Uncle Ross, I'm bleeding." Cray's voice is quavering, his hair matted with blood, eyes wild. But he's still standing.

I put my arm around him. "You're going to be okay," I say, not sure that it's true. Blood is gushing from his forehead and his front teeth are broken and terrible to see.

In the distance, flashing blue lights race toward us.

"Let's go," I say.

"Where?"

"Down there." I point at an alley next to a bar and we run as fast as we can, Cray limping. "Come on, we've really got to move," I shout.

"I think I'm about to pass out, Uncle Ross."

Sweat drips down my face. I keep one hand on Cray's shoulder to pull him ahead.

"It's hard to run," he says. "My ribs really hurt."

We come out of the alley and I look both ways, see no flashing lights. By the time we cross the street, sirens wail behind us.

"We're sunk," I whisper.

Cray shakes his head and points his chin at a stairway leading up. "Take my way, that's the skyway, that's the best," he
sings, then spits out a mouthful of blood.

We climb the stairs and find ourselves on a cement walkway
with scarred Plexiglas windows. The ground is littered with trash
and it smells of piss and cigarette smoke.

"Keep going straight, then take a left," Cray says. "Drops us
off right near the hotel."

We run down the skywalk, crossing the city along what must
have been an attempt to encourage downtown shopping. We try
to look normal, as though we're just blood-splattered shoppers
running flat out across the city before dawn.

We cut through a corporate atrium and tiptoe past a guard
sleeping facedown at his desk. We race across an empty arcade
and our footsteps echo like gunshots. The walkway stretches over
a street that I recognize. We're almost at the hotel. A squad car
races along the street beneath us. We drop to the gritty floor
and freeze as dozens of squad cars, sirens roaring, barrel toward the site of our unfortunate encounter with the local police.

"Can they see us up here?" Cray whispers.

I struggle to catch my breath. "Hope not."

"There's a lot of them."

"Policemen don't like it when you hurt one of their own."

"You think that cop is okay?"

"The one with the nightstick and gun and bad attitude?"

"That one."

"I think so," I say. "I just clipped him with the door."

"Nice move, by the way."

"It was the car, not me." I rise into a crouch, peer down on
the streets.

"Must be a special BMW feature," he says, words whistling through his broken teeth. "Uncle Ross, I think I left the Master Key in that last car."

I pause for a moment, absorb the news. "That's okay."

"Maybe you can get another one?"

"Sure." Malcolm told me that DMKs only come up every couple of years, BMW versions even less often. My career as a BMW converter is over for a while, maybe forever. Finally, the parade of police cars comes to an end.

"Let's go home," I say.

When we hear the knock, Cray and I walk together toward the door, me pressing the blood-soaked washcloth to his forehead, Cray struggling not to pass out.

I open the door and Marianne walks in, auburn hair disheveled. She's straightening her dress. "Whoa, this doesn't look good, boys."

"I didn't want to bother you," I say, "but I thought you might be handier with a needle and thread than I am."

Cray groans.

"Hit his head on the door frame, did he?" Marianne looks at me, waits to hear more. She's been awakened at dawn by a frantic phone call from a man she has known for a little over a week. She must think I'm crazy, or worse.

"We were stealing a car and got caught," I say, opting for honesty. "A cop beat Cray up."

"And what happened to the cop?"

"Uncle Ross ran him over with a BMW Bavaria," Cray mumbles.

"Not exactly," I say.

"And Malcolm told me you were such a mild-mannered pianist," Marianne says.

"Don't be so sure about that," Cray slurs. "Ask him about his diamond collection."

I nudge Cray. Marianne says nothing.

Marianne and I work as a team, carefully layering the floor with towels, then helping Cray down. While I upend a tiny bourbon from the minibar into Cray's smashed mouth, Marianne comes back with the sewing kit from the bathroom. She threads the needle while I hold ice on the cut along his hairline. I pull away and Marianne leans over Cray for about a minute, singing to him quietly as she sews, *Walking After Midnight*. Before she even gets to the second chorus, she bends forward as if to kiss Cray's forehead, then bites off the thread.

"Where'd you learn to do that?"

"Mom's bar back in Florida was a gun-and-knife kind of place. That's where I learned how to sing, stitch up drunk college kids, and other useful life skills." Marianne tapes a small white bandage over the stitching, cleans away the remaining blood, then steps back to admire her work.

"Like new, kind of," she says.

Cray rises slowly, walks over to the mirror. "That hurt a lot," he says, holding back his hair to see the results. "But not as much as my mouth." He smiles, revealing broken teeth, bleeding gums.

"Not much we can do for the teeth. I don't expect you brought the pieces with you."

"They're somewhere down on Fourth Street," I say.

"Just keep ice in your mouth for a couple of hours," Marianne says. "And probably some whiskey too. Eventually, you'll need to go to a dentist, but not around here. They're probably looking for someone to turn up in the ER."

"So what do I do, just hide in the hotel room?"

Marianne shakes her head. "You need to get out of town, sooner the better."

"Any particular plan in mind?" I ask. Marianne is proving to be unflappable in the face of this bloody debacle, a rare quality in upper-tier hotel singers.

"I may have just the thing," she says. "Wait here."

While Cray lies on the bed, I clean up our suite so it no longer looks like an operating room. I fold up the bloody towels and shove them in a plastic laundry bag.

"Sounds like I'm leaving, Uncle Ross."

I nod my head. "You said you wanted to go home. Careful what you wish for."

"I'm real sorry," he says softly.

"It's not your fault," I say. "Well, actually—it is."

"I know."

"Listen, you have to slow down, Cray. Almost everything works better if you pull the tempo down a notch."

"I'll remember that if I start playing piano."

"I'm not talking about playing the piano."

There's a soft knock on the door and I open it cautiously, let Marianne in. Over her arm she carries a full Army dress uniform, brass buttons gleaming. "Here you go, soldier boy," she says. She hands Cray the uniform, then unfolds a regulation black beret that she slides gently over his hair, neatly covering his bandage.

"Go put this on and we'll get you out of here."

Cray walks into the bedroom.

"There'll be a lot of very angry cops downtown," she says. "But I should be able to get him over to the bus station. He can get on a bus back to Vermont. No one will question a soldier."

"Where'd you get that uniform?"

"There's a recruiting office a couple doors down the street."

"Isn't it closed this early in the morning?"

"Let's just say that one of my biggest admirers in Cincinnati is part of the military-industrial complex." She holds her hand up, palm out. "No more questions. Time to hit the road."

Cray walks back in looking surprisingly ready for duty.

"I love a man in uniform," Marianne says.

"Apparently," I whisper.

"Heard that."

"Better pack up your things," I say to Cray.

Marianne shakes her head. "No, leave it. Travel light. Don't bring anything that might look suspicious."

"Like a duffel bag full of counterfeit twenty-dollar bills?" Cray asks.

"Yes, like that."

Cray nods. We walk toward the door.

"Not so fast, handsome," Marianne says to me. "You better stay here. They may have gotten a good look at you. No one will be looking for a woman and her young, enlisted boyfriend."

Marianne puts her arms around me and gives me a gentle kiss. "We'll talk later."

Cray stumbles down the hallway.

"Call when you get home, Cray," I say, then realize how annoyingly maternal it sounds. I close the door and lean against it for a moment, my face against the cool metal. I see the fire diagram, a red arrow marking the safe way out. If only escape could be that easy.

philadelphia

Admirers cluster around Marianne, enthralled by every note she sings. I sit in the back of the Fountain Room, amazed and annoyed by her fans. At the end of *Moonlight,* the pack of geezers applauds wildly. There are no wives, no girlfriends—just a fraternity of aging businessmen vying for her attentions.

I'm more than a little jealous. After the Cincinnati incident, Marianne's been keeping her distance. Cray probably told her something terrible and fictional about me. Or she doesn't want to get involved with a car thief, which is all I am to her now. This chilling of her affections makes me want her even more, a reaction that I find way too conventional. *Men want what they can't have. And when they get what they want, they don't want it anymore.* I'd like to think I've evolved beyond clichés, but apparently I haven't.

"Are you having dinner tonight?" my waiter asks for the second time.

"No, I'm here with . . ." I point toward Marianne.

He raises his eyebrows. "Oh. Well, can I get you another glass of wine?"

"Yes." I nod.

"I'll add it to Marianne's tab—she drinks for free here," he says. "Wonderful woman, Miss London . . ."

The waiter drifts away, buoyed by thoughts of Marianne's loveliness. I wonder for a moment if she is leading on every man in the world, including me. We've been on the road together for a while now. I played piano for Marianne during a couple of her gigs. She dropped in to do a couple of numbers with me when I played the Sheraton in Pittsburgh. We travel together in Marianne's car, splitting the driving. We stay up late talking in hotel bars. But somehow, though we're on the same circuit now, we end up in our own rooms every night. And it's starting to bother me.

The crowd rises up to clap along in the spastic, arrhythmic way of white men as Marianne sings *Lush Life.*

Though I could be falling in love with Marianne, I can still say objectively that her singing voice is beautiful. She reminds me a little of Connee Boswell, always staying in the lower registers, never venturing too high, exactly the opposite of most club singers. It's a siren song for wealthy, well-tended men. I watch tonight's admirers and wonder which one will be giving Marianne some kind of expensive jewelry tonight, pouring her champagne in his hotel room. But my shadow life doesn't leave me much room to criticize the way Marianne chooses to spend her evenings. Maybe that's the way she likes it—lots of admirers, no real love.

When I told her about Alta, my last girlfriend, Marianne was brutal. "Sounds like a greedy girl with good taste. Anyway, what did you expect?" she said. "Falling in love always starts with fire and ends with ice. If it was the other way around, no one would even bother."

And apparently that's what we're doing now, not even bothering, knowing the true course of love. Failed romance could be an occupational hazard. All of the songs in our collective fakebook are clear on the impossibility of love that lasts.

The set ends, the crowd applauds wildly, then the restaurant returns to the buzz of conversation and the occasional burst of fire from a flaming dessert. I already finished an uneventful one-night gig at Chez Colette, playing a set for rich people who wouldn't know Monk from punk. I tell myself that vocalists are always more popular than pianists, particularly beautiful singers who know a few tricks.

Marianne revealed some of her stage tips to me during our long drives. "I wear tight, shiny dresses and bras that could give an eight-year-old cleavage. I lean over a lot. I look every man in the audience directly in the eye at some point during the show, and this convinces them that I *want them*. I joke about not having anyone in my life. And I spray on some perfume made from bee pheromones. If I sing a song about being lonely, I work up a tear, then brush it away when they applaud. I gaze at them gratefully, leave the stage, and wait to see who shows up in my dressing room, who sends flowers." She passed along these tips as dispassionately as a machinist describing the best settings for a metal lathe. Delmar Robbins would be proud.

At the time, I was struck by how obvious her ploys were. But now that I see Marianne in action, I realize she is a consummate pro. I have the piano to hide behind. Marianne only has her voice, but she's captivating and in charge. She bends forward slightly at the waist, pushing her full lips down toward the microphone, held gently in both hands, but never quite touching it. Sometimes a microphone is more than a microphone, as Marianne pointed out, and Dr. Freud would second. She finishes singing, and manages to tear herself away from her crowd to drop by my table.

She leans over and kisses me, then puts her lips next to my ear. "Room 2304, in about an hour," she whispers. And then she's gone, swept back up in the laughter and admirers. Something's shifted and thawed and I'm alive again, stirred by the possibilities, despite all the delays and cautions.

Exactly an hour later, I'm at Room 2304, my hand shaking as I raise it to knock on the door. I've been at the hotel room doors of hundreds of women—wives of senators, women who run major corporations, women with clout, money, and very large diamonds. But something more powerful than the promise of diamonds has drawn me to Room 2304.

Marianne opens the door gently. She's wearing the plush hotel robe, open to the waist. In the darkened room behind her, a candle burns next to a bottle of champagne chilling on the nightstand.

"Been waiting for you," Marianne says. "For a long time." She kisses me, a repeat of that first, unexpected kiss in her car.

She presses her cheek against my shoulder. "I know I've been strange lately. It's just that . . . well, I kind of got used to not caring about anyone. Then you come along. It's complicated."

I kiss her on the ear, then whisper in it. "If we just played the easy songs over and over, we'd get bored. Sometimes you have to try something new and strange."

"Exactly. There's something I want to show you," she whispers. "I think you'll like it. Definitely new and strange."

Marianne leads me into the bedroom and clicks on the overhead lights, revealing an enormous naked dead man lying face-up on the bed.

"*Ta da!*" she says, waving her arm with a flourish.

Stunned, I say nothing at first.

"He's not dead," she says. "Just very, very, very asleep." She takes my hand and leads me over to the side of the bed.

"This is something I'm supposed to like?"

"Well, you got to admit it's interesting. And strange. Just look at him," she says. "Cal Ruderman, president of American Fruit. Lives in a town house on Chestnut Street. Winters in Boca Raton. Giant yacht. Collection of vintage cars. Known for being a tough businessman. *Forbes* calls him *Top Banana,* which he likes a lot, by the way."

We gaze down as if viewing an educational diorama—EARLY 21ST-CENTURY POWER MONGER IN HIS HABITAT. Ruderman's skin is awash with constellations of moles, small scars, blotches. His chest is covered with a thick mat of gray hair. Between his legs, his lanky penis is sheathed in a bright yellow condom.

"It's like looking at a dinosaur," she says. "Years from now, we can say we saw the last of the species."

I break the educational spell. "Marianne, why is this naked man here?"

"It's his room."

"And the yellow condom?"

"He thinks it's funny. You can imagine the banana jokes. But lucky for me, he always fades before I have to do anything with that damn banana."

"How's that?"

Marianne reaches into the pocket of her robe and holds up a prescription bottle. She opens it and shakes out a small triangular blue pill. "Recognize this, grandfather's little helper?"

I nod.

"High-test barbiturate tablets repackaged to look like horn-candy. Knocks them to their knees on the way back from the bathroom."

"I thought you were straight, that your admirers just gave you presents."

"They do, but I take some things too." Marianne walks over to the desk, where the comatose Top Banana's trousers are carefully folded over the back of the chair. She takes out his thick wallet and flips through the credit cards like a croupier.

"American Express Centurion Black—that's about as good as it gets, five hundred dollars on the aftermarket. And a couple of the other ones are pretty nice." She takes out a small silver device slightly smaller than an electric shaver and slides it over each card.

"What's that thing?"

"Digital scanner. It's wireless. Beams the numbers right to my laptop downstairs." She flips the cards and scans the reverse sides, taking care with the signatures. "There, my hard work is done." She sighs, pockets the scanner, then carefully replaces the cards in the wallet, the wallet in the pants.

"I call it a *creditectomy*. I get their license, credit cards,

Social Security number, signature, address. Everything someone needs to get a nice line of credit, make some major purchases, max out the cash advances, and disappear. Bankers call it *credit card bust-out.*"

"You do all that?"

"No, silly. That's for the pros, guys sitting in front of computer terminals in the Netherlands Antilles. I just send along the data and get paid for it. Like I said, my work is over."

I'm seeing a new side of Marianne. Her latest admirer squirms a little and emits a feral grunt. "Maybe not," I whisper.

She reaches down to pick up his banana and give it a jiggle. She shakes her head. "No, he's still lost in the jungle."

For weeks, I worried what Marianne might think about my nightwork with all its messy writhing. Now it turns out that she's channeling desire into revenue too. But how far does she have to go to get it?

"Do you have sex with them?" The question pops out of my mouth.

She shrugs. "Depends on what you call sex. After they wake up, I just tell them how great they were. That's generally enough. And if they still have the urge, a little almond oil and a couple of strokes with my right hand usually finishes them off. You know what I've learned in all these years?"

"I'm not sure I want to know."

Marianne rolls her eyes. "Telling each other secrets is how we learn to trust each other, Ross."

"Okay, you go first."

"My admirers don't want to have sex. The older they get, the less they care about the gymnastics. It's all phony, anyway. A business tiger like this one? He'd rather be entering new markets than entering me."

Marianne gives her admirers—or as someone more litigious might call them, victims—what they want. Romance, or at least the false hope of it. Then she takes something she needs. It sounds familiar, really familiar.

"What about you?" Marianne sits on the bed next to the banana baron and he rolls toward her. She shoves him back into the middle. "Do you fuck them?"

"I don't have any admirers."

"That's not what Cray told me."

Now Marianne's chilliness on the road makes sense. Cray told her about the other women to scare her off. And it worked.

"Okay, I've been known to spend time with women in their hotel rooms. But we don't *do it,* at least not in the usual way. And I don't drug them, either, by the way."

"You just bring them back to the hotel room and give them a peck on the cheek?"

"No, I listen to them. And touch them."

"You touch them." Marianne's eyebrows rise a bit.

"Yes. For a long time."

"You don't actually have sex with them?"

I shake my head. "No."

"Why not?"

"The same reason you don't, probably."

"They disgust you?"

"No. It doesn't seem fair to steal something from them and to take advantage of them too."

Marianne squints. "You steal something from them?"

"I take their diamonds. Actually, I replace them with fakes."

Marianne laughs. "Cray didn't tell me that. But I should have figured it out. Stealing diamonds requires some steady nerves. Fast hands, too." She narrows her eyes and summons up a detail.

"I used to open for a magician in Boston who claimed to have the fastest hands in the world—Mr. Fingers. I'm going to have to call you that from now on."

Marianne reaches out and takes my hand, puts the tip of my index finger on her lips. Then she brings my hand under her robe, first to her breast, next lower. My hand moves with a mind of its own, seeking out the delicate places to stroke, to press.

Her hands are just as busy, unfastening my belt, loosening my pants.

She sighs a little. "Touch me, Mr. Fingers."

"Don't call me that."

"Mr. Fingers!" Marianne's shout stirs the Banana Man. She hops down on the floor, unfastens her robe, and waves me toward her. I see her dark, wide nipples, narrow hips, delicate cleft. "Come here. I have a diamond hidden somewhere. See if you can find it."

I shake my head.

"Scared of the big naked man in the bed?"

"A little."

"You're a pro. Figure out some way for the show to go on."

"Let's go into the bathroom," I say.

Marianne shakes her head. "A real lady doesn't do it bent over the sink in the bathroom like a fifty-dollar whore."

"But she can drag home old men, drug them, and scan their credit cards."

She shrugs. "You're so *twentieth-century*, Mr. Fingers."

I reach my hand down to bring her back to her feet. Instead, she pulls me down toward her. Gracelessly, I stumble down to my knees on the carpet, my pants half-down, then lurch forward. Marianne catches me and I plunge inside her, unceremoniously, urgently.

"*There,*" she says. "I've been wanting you for a long time. Inside me. All the way."

I say nothing, just hold still, feel Marianne's warmth around me. I press my eyes closed. It's been years since I let myself get this close, to break down the distance between bodies until none is left. It feels so incredibly good and right.

Then I hear the water running in the bathroom.

Marianne pushes me away. "Jesus, he's awake!"

The once-comatose Cal Ruderman stands in the bright bathroom, one hand on the wall, the other peeling his banana. Soon a thin trickle is heading in the general direction of the toilet.

"I think he may be *sleep-peeing.*"

"Get going, Ross. Now." Marianne pushes me toward the door. I gather my clothes on the way, leaving the room just as Banana Man staggers in from the bathroom.

The door clicks closed. I put on my underwear and shirt in the hallway, then realize that my pants are still inside. My room key is in my pocket. I think about knocking but decide it wouldn't be a good idea. Instead, I walk to the elevator, looking elegant from the waist up, almost naked below. My black German dress shoes look ridiculous without socks, pants.

Miles Davis never looked so stupid.

The elevator door opens, revealing a room service cart and behind it, a bell captain in full uniform, gold epaulettes, and white gloves.

"Good evening, sir."

I nod.

"What floor?"

"Eighteen."

He presses the button and it lights up. We travel up in silence. We reach my floor and the door slides open.

"You seem to have misplaced your pants, sir. Will you be needing a new key to get into your room?"

His politeness is admirable, ridiculous.

"Yes. Thank you for asking."

He clicks the HOLD button on the elevator and escorts me to my room. At the door, he takes out a key and waves it in front of the lock, which clicks green and opens. The DMK of hotel rooms. I want one.

"Thanks," I say. "Wait for just a moment." I walk inside and find my fakebook, take out five $100 bills. I fold them into my palm and walk back to the door, hand the cash to the bell captain without a word. He looks me in the eye for a moment, smiles slightly.

Discretion does not come cheap, but I'm more than willing to pay the price tonight.

I spot Marianne every now and then during our time in Philadelphia. We've been disconnected ever since our furtive coupling next to Banana Man's bed. I know too much about what goes into her work. She's having breakfast in the hotel restaurant with a guy I recognize from CNN. She flashes by in her gray Mercedes, piloted by another admirer. She calls my room before her second set, tells me that she misses me, but that she's very busy—that she has to *make hay while the sun shines*. Her call doesn't reassure me. I know it's not hay she's making.

The thought of her in bed next to a naked admirer, even one in a drug-induced stupor, makes me furious, then embarrassed for it. Who am I to be jealous?

I skip Marianne's shows. Her eager admirers make me angry.

It's hard not to imagine a steady stream of them striding naked through Marianne's hotel room in all their preening, wattle-assed glory. Instead of walking downstairs to catch her second set, I sit in my hotel room and stare out the window at the sunset, waiting for the transcendence of overwhelming beauty to sweep over me. Ten minutes later, I realize I'm simply staring out the window like someone with nothing better to do than to watch the sun going down over Philadelphia.

The phone rings and breaks me out of my trance.

"Uncle Ross!"

"Cray?" I'm surprised to hear his voice again, even more surprised to find that I'm glad to hear from him.

"What are you doing, Uncle Ross?"

"Eating a burrito. Washing it down with an Amstel Light."

"That's so freaky, Uncle Ross. That's exactly what I had for dinner."

"Clearly, we both have fine taste."

A pause. "I miss driving around with you, Uncle Ross."

"Me too," I say. Our time together seems decades earlier and far simpler. Marianne's arrival has changed everything. "How are things there?"

"Dad's on the warpath. You probably shouldn't talk to him for a while."

I say nothing. "Why?"

"He thinks it's your fault that I got the shit kicked out of me by that cop."

"You're not exactly easy to keep an eye on, Cray."

"I know. But he's really pissed off about my teeth. I think he's sending you the bill."

"How are your teeth?"

"Got them replaced with gold ones, Uncle Ross. All my friends want to get their teeth whacked out now. I told them it's not such a good idea."

"Your father cracked a tooth off once when we were kids." I remember how we stole a dessert cart from a fancy restaurant, handed out cake to bums, then rode the cart downhill until Ray fell off and smacked his face on Michigan Avenue.

"He told me," Cray says. "He caught a guy stealing his car in Chicago once and had to smack him around. Right, Uncle Ross?"

"Sure." I wonder if there is a limit to how far the truth can be stretched.

"You coming up this way?" Cray asks.

"We're in New York, Providence, then Boston. You could drive down when we're in Boston, show me your gold teeth and everything." I glance at my watch. Marianne is halfway through her first set by now.

"What do you mean, we?"

"Marianne and I—we're sort of traveling together."

"Like we traveled together?"

"Not exactly."

"I don't know about her, Uncle Ross. I didn't get a great feeling about her. I think she's up to something."

"She's definitely up to something. But it's okay."

A pause. "You're in love, aren't you, Uncle Ross?"

"No. I'm in *like*. Marianne and I have a lot in common, Cray. More than I knew. We're both strange as three-dollar bills."

"There is no three-dollar bill, Uncle Ross. Believe me, if there were I'd know about it. Got to run. Dad says two minutes on the pay phone is the max. Otherwise, They start tracing. Guess I shouldn't say that. Anyway, see you around, I hope."

The phone clicks off.

I used to have hours on my own, days even. But now time away from Marianne has changed *being alone* into *being lonely*.

I know of only one antidote. I grab a stack of hundreds from the back of my fakebook—real cash, not Ray's version—and take the elevator downstairs.

The crowd sounds echo across the lobby from the Fountain Room, Marianne's voice entwined among the laughter and talking. She's singing a Sarah Vaughan number, *Dancing in the Dark,* which I know she'll follow with *Ain't No Use* and then *The Man I Love,* finishing up with *He's Funny That Way,* the Billie Holiday version.

I walk by the reception desk and into the cool night, past the somber parking lot attendants in ludicrous British uniforms. I'm invisible, a man in a dark suit who seems to know where he's going, who requires no downtown map or restaurant advice.

I walk until I come to a neighborhood where the streets are darker, the brick apartment buildings less quaint. I could go door to door with the cash, pushing a hundred into every mail slot. But that's too risky. Instead, I walk along the street, peeling off a bill every few yards and letting it drop by my side. Some bills skid along the road on a gentle breeze. Others lose themselves under battered cars. The bills mean no more to me than the early leaves in the gutters.

After a few blocks, the stack of cash dwindles to a few final hundreds, which I tuck under the windshield wiper of a brown Dodge.

I turn and look for a moment at the street I've seeded with cash, wait for the moment to arrive, the one that tells me I've done something good and strange that will be appreciated and talked about for years. *Remember when we woke up one morning and found money swirling down the street?* Scraps of high-value paper skitter across the pavement beneath a sputtering streetlight.

I shiver in the cool breeze, then turn to walk back to my hotel, my footsteps along the gritty street accompanied by a barking dog, a siren in the distance.

We drive, leaving Philadelphia in near silence, Marianne at the wheel, me watching the woods fly by at eighty miles an hour. The summer is coming undone, mid-September heat giving way to cool mornings. The fields are mounded with bales of hay, and the yellowed vines along their borders hang heavy with wolf grapes. Ray and I used to search for them when we were kids, then ferment the juice in the basement and sell the "wine" for a dollar a bottle. Another scam from our repertoire.

Marianne drinks from a paper cup of coffee, her delicate throat wavering slightly when she swallows. I want to run my tongue along her neck and wonder if an admirer has been doing exactly that last night.

"You can't be mad at me for doing what I do," she says, breaking the silence, reading my mind.

"You mean singing in nightclubs?"

"No, the other thing I do."

"Luring old rich men with your many charms, drugging them, and stealing their identities?"

"Yes, that."

"Sure I'm mad about it," I say. "It was a complete surprise. And it definitely changes things between us."

"What do you mean?"

"You know what I mean. Your admirers creep me out."

"Me too, believe me."

"I'm not sure I do anymore."

"Oh yeah? Well what about your special lady friends? The ones you diddle for diamonds. They don't exactly make me happy either, you know." Marianne shakes her head. "We have to work this out, Ross, if we're going to keep . . ."

"Traveling together?" I take off my sunglasses, move my hand over to her thigh, run my fingers along her black silk slip.

"Yes, traveling together." Marianne closes her eyes for a moment, then opens them again. "Move your hand unless you want us to wind up wrapped around a tree."

I run my hand beneath her slip, trace my fingers along the delicate curve of her leg, starting at her knee and moving up.

Marianne grabs my hand, carefully lifts it away from her leg and places it on the leather seat between us. "Hands to yourself, Mr. Fingers."

"Do you say that to your admirers?"

Marianne turns and squints at me. "You're jealous, aren't you? Jealous of the geezers I steal from?"

"Well, not when you put it that way."

"Because that's ridiculous, Ross. They're just a way for me to get money quick and easy."

"I've seen you walking through the crowd during your gigs, touching each of them, looking like they mean the world to you."

"And they did for a couple of hours. That's about how long it takes me to hook them solid, Ross. Then it's up to their room for . . ."

"Spare me the details, Marianne."

"But you already know. They drink some Scotch to wash down the fake Viagra. Then there are a few bleary minutes of stupid talk and inept groping, maybe followed by a handjob.

Then they fall into a narco-coma for an hour while I go through their wallets and make their credit rating a living hell for six months or so. Is that what you're jealous of, Ross?"

I say nothing.

"Meanwhile, you're off in another hotel room with your fingers roaming free into the nether regions of women you hardly know like some kind of freelance gynecologist."

"Means nothing to me," I say.

"Exactly," she says. "We're both just supplementing our incomes in creative ways. Just like Malcolm encourages us to."

"As if you needed encouragement."

"You're not getting it, Ross. You and I both steal from people late at night. You take their diamonds, I take their data. In exchange, they get a few minutes of pleasure."

"Except you seem to enjoy it, Marianne," I say. "I've seen you with them, and I have to say, you don't exactly look like you're dreading the whole thing."

"Well, who are you to judge whether I'm enjoying it or faking it? I sure wouldn't be the first woman to pretend that spending time with men was actually fun when it isn't. And I can fake an orgasm that you can hear for miles."

She begins with low breathing, a husky *"Oh God!,"* then, more urgently, a sharp intake of breath, blurted words, primal growls, and then concludes a minute later with a long sigh.

"Was it as good for you as it was for me?" she says flatly, then reaches over to press her hand in my own nether regions, finding that her work found a receptive audience. "Ha! You knew I was faking and it still fooled you, Ross. Even you."

I pull away. "How am I supposed to believe anything you say, anything about you?"

Marianne accelerates smoothly, takes the exit that leads us to

New York City. "Well, like so many other things, Ross, you just need to have a bit of faith. I haven't done anything so far to make you feel like you can't trust me, have I?"

I shake my head. "Of course not."

"Then I think we'll both just have to learn how to leave our work at the office. Because we both need the extra money. My mother's bills are not going to be paid off by hotel gigs alone."

I stare out the window.

Marianne looks over at me. "What do you do with it?"

"With what?"

"The extra money. You're not exactly living in luxury."

I look her in the eye. "I give it away."

"To help your father? Or your family? Is that what you mean?"

"No. They don't need any help. I give it away to strangers."

"What?"

"I give the money away."

"You mean you give some of it away. Like the way rich people give a little to charity to make themselves feel better, right?"

"No. I give away the money I make from stealing."

"And how much is that?"

I shake my head. "I don't really keep track of it."

"You've been doing this for how long?"

"For years."

The Mercedes skids into the emergency lane and comes to an abrupt stop. Cars honk as they rush past.

"Then we're talking about hundreds of thousands of dollars, Ross, right?"

"More like millions." I tell her about my Send BMWs to China program.

"You've given away millions of dollars to people that you don't even know?" She shakes her head.

"Right."

"And you don't even keep a little bit for yourself?"

"No."

"That's crazy."

I shrug. "I don't think so."

"So why do you do it?"

"I don't need the money. Other people do. It's that simple."

"You *steal from the rich and give to the poor.*" Marianne seems stunned.

"I'm good at turning stupid expensive things into cash really quickly. It's a gift. And I figure I should use it. Wealth's getting too concentrated. Someone's got to help spread it around."

"That's why you give away the money?"

"In a macro sense, yes."

"Last time I checked, people don't really live at the macro level, Ross. There's got to be more to it than that."

I pause, watch cars rushing by on their way to New York. "It's a thrill to be able to do something well. I like playing the piano. You like to sing. We do it because we're really good at it. Same thing."

"Maybe," Marianne says. "But we also do it because we get paid. And I don't think there's anyone else out on the circuit who gives away their money. They've all got something they need money for—an apartment in New York, nice cars, fine wine, a kid in college, a drug habit."

"Don't get me wrong. I used to spend it all. I bought a nice loft, a Bösendorfer grand, and a $3,000 cat with an eating disorder."

"I thought you hated pets."

"I do now. Anyway, one day I just gave up on it all."

"Why?"

"The truth?"

"Sure."

"It bored me. All that thinking about buying, deciding what to buy, the actual buying. It took a lot of time and made me miserable. It reminded me of the way Chief always wanted the next big thing, the new job, the big payoff. And look how that turned out. Cancer and cronies. Now I don't want anything."

"Don't you want me?" she says, pretending to be offended.

"Of course I do. But I'm not paying a cent."

"And I'm not charging you. I'd jump you right here on the highway, but we might attract the attention of the state police. And I don't think either of us want that."

She knocks the Mercedes into gear and pulls out into the river of afternoon traffic.

"A week in New York," she says after a few minutes. "I want a week alone with you. Might help you learn how to love again. And me too. Where are you playing?"

"Hotel Elysée, Monkey Bar."

"I'm at the Waldorf for a couple of nights. Then we don't have a gig until Providence. We'll disappear for a little bit, just you and me. Forget about our day jobs. And our night jobs. No one else around. No cell phones. Just us. What do you say?"

I think of Chet Baker, who used to shoot up and drive aimlessly up the California coast with a beautiful girlfriend next to him in the convertible. "We'll get lost."

"Yes," Marianne says. "We'll get very lost. Then found. Then lost again."

new york city

Marianne's suite in the Waldorf Towers has six rooms, a view of St. Bartholomew's, and a grand piano in the living room. The bellboy shows us around, opens closets, turns on lights, all to make sure we're pleased. He tells us that the Secretary of State stays here. Ten minutes and a $100 tip later, we're alone.

If Cray were providing the account of our week together in this penthouse suite, he would rush to what he considered the good parts—sex in front of the TV, a dinner of burritos, more sex, then a postcoital Amstel Light. But that's not the way it goes.

We play our gigs and push each other to work the audience—not for diamonds or solid-gold credit, but just because we can. Each night ends with sweat and crowds and applause, not in the hotel rooms of strangers.

Saturday night finds us in our enormous bed, exhausted, ears ringing. We sleep together with more tenderness than passion—we're tired. Sunday morning, the sky over Manhattan is blue and empty. Bright sunlight slants across our rooms. Down on the streets, students are coming back to college, people are out shopping and buying and spending. But we stay alone in our bed high above the city, a new couple finding our way.

"Why were you so shy with this?" Marianne throws back the covers and runs her hand up my thigh, takes me in her hand like a microphone. "Always denying your special lady friends the real action, just giving them your patented Mr. Fingers act."

I pull away and yank the covers back up. "I was waiting for you to come along."

"Thanks, but not good enough."

"I didn't want to leave a trail of young Wolfsheads along the road. You met Cray—can you imagine more of him?"

"Better, but you're still not being honest."

"Because I'm shy?"

"You play piano in front of hundreds of strangers and you're worried about a little traditional sex?"

"I don't want to owe anyone anything," I say finally. "Every act is a transaction, an exchange. Even sex. Particularly sex."

"That sounds more like it," Marianne says. "But here's what I think, Ross. Here's what I think is at the core of your Mr. Fingers routine. You're scared."

"Scared?" I shift a little in the bed, rest my right ear between her breasts, hear her heart beating.

"Yes, scared. I'm not sure of what—maybe your parents' crappy marriage or your greedy girlfriend—what was her name again, Alto?"

"Alta."

"Anyway, maybe she put you off the whole love thing. We'll leave that for a professional. But for now, I know you like being an outsider. You're always talking about Miles Davis. He's the ultimate outsider."

"Actually, I think he managed to find his way inside a lot of willing women. Read the autobiography."

"What I'm saying is this, Ross. Your days as an outsider are over."

"And why's that?"

"Because I'm going to cure you." Marianne smiles, then climbs out of bed. Perhaps it's her free-spirited upbringing in sunny Florida, but Marianne is completely comfortable wandering around naked. She strides around the suite, opens a drawer, takes out a paperback, then another.

"*Bibliocoitus,*" she says when she crawls back into bed.

I give her a blank look.

"Sex with books."

"Doesn't that kind of stick the pages together?"

"Very funny, but that's not what I mean." Marianne turns away, dovetailing against me. "Here, take your medicine." She hands me a copy of *Beyond the Horizon,* the biography of Conrad Hilton, founder of the Hilton Hotel chain, a paperback left in every room of the Waldorf to replace Gideon's Bible, apparently.

"I've been waiting to read this for years," I say. "Please don't tell me how it ends. Wait a minute—I bet he gets rich and dies, right?"

"Don't think of it as a book," she says. "It's like an eye chart, something to stare at, while . . ."

"While what?"

"While this." Marianne presses close to me, both of us facing the row of windows that looks out on a gleaming Byzantine syringe of an office building rising above St. Bart's. She reaches back to take me in her hand, guides me. I press slowly inside with a gasp.

"There," she says. "Now read."

"But I don't want to read now."

"I want you inside me as long as possible," she says. "Everyone has it all wrong. Lingerie? Performance-enhancing drugs? They just speed up the act. But the right reading material can slow it way, way down." Marianne takes out her book, *Be My Guest,* Conrad Hilton's autobiography, also provided free with the room as part of the all-Hilton library.

I struggle to focus on the pages in front of me. I'm moving very slowly inside Marianne, who pushes against me in a delicate rhythm.

"You need to be reading something incredibly boring. That way you can postpone the inevitable until . . ." Marianne gazes over at the clock on the night table. It's ten o'clock. "Until about noon. We'll order lunch to celebrate. With champagne! But for now, focus, Ross. I've seen your intense powers of concentration. Time to put them to the test."

I dutifully open my book and read about Conrad Hilton's Norwegian father, his German mother, and his strong belief in the American dream. The preface is short, but I find myself skipping ahead. "It says here that Hilton was convinced that there is a natural law that obliges all mankind to help relieve the suffering, distressed, and destitute."

"Sounds familiar," Marianne says. "In the autobiography, he comes off a lot more arrogant."

Marianne presses slowly against me and I close my eyes.

"Just read," I say. "And hold still, please."

We read on silently, or nearly so, for about an hour. We work our way through Conrad's early years at St. Michael's College in Santa Fe, the thrill of buying his first hotel in 1919—the Mobley Hotel in Cisco, Texas. The construction of the Dallas Hilton in 1925 was difficult, but not nearly as difficult as having sex in slow motion. Thankfully, I come to a bleak passage about the Great Depression, which reminds me of Chief's stories about his own Dust Bowl boyhood. I read about Conrad's obsession with efficiency and keeping costs low and quality high. It's an inspiring read, I suppose, and it's serving its purpose well. The clock grinds toward eleven o'clock. Conrad still only owns a handful of hotels and Marianne and I are already damp with sweat.

We're both breathing quickly as we squint at the pages of the cheap paperbacks in our shaking hands.

Half an hour later, Conrad has expanded his empire to include the Sir Francis Drake in San Francisco, the Plaza in New York, the Stevens, the Palmer House, the Waldorf-Astoria. I played a couple of gigs at the Palmer House and I try to distract myself by remembering the room, whether the crowds were good, how much I was paid.

"Are you up to the part where he marries Zsa Zsa?" Marianne says through clenched teeth.

"You've been skimming."

"So what?"

"I'm reading about his efforts to use advertising to promote world peace through international trade and travel."

"Boring."

"Maybe not quite enough." I look at the clock. Fifteen minutes until noon. "How do I know that you haven't, you know . . . ?"

"*Achieved success,* as the French say?"

"Yes, that."

"Believe me, you'll know. All of Midtown will know. Tell me about something dull from your childhood," Marianne says, eyes pinched closed. "Make it boring."

"My brother and I used to spend hours at bookstores when we were kids," I say, taking a break from Conrad and his own relentless march to success. "Our favorite was in Evanston. A place called City of Books. One city block, three floors, all packed with used books."

"Were all the books dull?"

"Yes, they were very, very dull. Ray tended to get lost in the typography section and the coin books. Roman coins. Price guides. I read history books, musician biographies, crime novels that smelled like wet newspapers."

Marianne nods quickly. "Tell me more. Make it really, really boring."

"We'd sit in the store for hours, the air around us sparkling with dust, reading, never saying much, just reading like little weird animals hungry for facts," I say. "It was the closest I ever felt to anyone in my family."

"You should go visit your brother. See how Cray's doing. Maybe we'll drive up to see him after we finish having sex . . . I mean, after we finish this tour."

"I don't think Ray wants visitors. He's definitely a solo kind of guy. Plus, he's not particularly happy with me."

"Why?"

"Cray's little accident."

"Oh. Well, that wasn't exactly your fault."

"I was supposed to be watching him."

"A watched pot never boils."

"I have no idea what you mean by that."

"Me neither. I'm just talking." Marianne looks at the clock. "Only five more minutes. Can you make it?"

I nod. "Back to our reading."

Marianne dutifully opens her paperback. I read the last section of mine, which covers the post-Conrad era of the Hilton empire. Conrad's son Nicky marries Elizabeth Taylor for a year. There's a picture of Taylor with her legendary cleavage. I turn the page quickly. I read about his son Barron, who by the year 2000 owned more than five hundred hotels around the world. I skip the section on infamous celebutard Paris Hilton and her ninny sister.

Instead, I try to remember all the Hilton hotels I've stayed in, a version of counting sheep that allows me to forget for a moment that I'm in the final stages of a prolonged sexual act, one that's drawing to a tumultuous finale.

"Twelve noon—it's time," Marianne shouts.

We toss our books on the floor. Marianne pushes hard against me until we merge into the beast with one back. I wrap my arms around her, crossing them, hands cupping an opposite breast, fingertips pressed gently over her nipples. We shut our eyes tightly. Looking at our faces, you might think we were falling from an airplane or enduring simultaneous outpatient surgery. We writhe together, closer, until our tower suite echoes with a duet of gasps, screams, then sighs, all in harmony.

That moment, I become a confirmed insider.

In the calm and exhaustion that follows, I take the lobe of

Marianne's ear and press it gently between my teeth, then run my finger across her lips. They move slowly, as if she were speaking to someone, telling the story of what just happened, as if by repeating it we could relive it again and again.

Marianne and I stay in our suite, playing piano and "reading for pleasure." At night, we leave the hotel only for dinners at the latest one-word restaurants—Envy, Eon, Burn—long meals with meandering, wine-fueled conversations that go on until three in the morning. We wander through Central Park and I give away the occasional Jackson to one of the stunned-looking outdoorsmen sprawled near the Reflecting Pool.

The first day of October finds us sitting on a bench on Fifth Avenue just south of the museums, the warm sun on our faces.

"I think I know why you give away money," Marianne says softly. She's been strangely quiet all morning.

"Why?"

"Because you don't really care about money," she says. "Otherwise you'd be scurrying down the street to some job." She points around us, at the dozens of people rushing to work, earbudded, cell-phoned, and oblivious to the morning sun stealing through the city block by block.

"Maybe I just care more about giving it away than keeping it."

"That sounds good, Ross. And if I were writing a feature article on your *Robin Hood meets Bill Evans* act, that would be a great quote."

I laugh uneasily, not sure where Marianne's going with this.

"You're just giving away something that means nothing to you, the way people put stuff out on the sidewalk with a FREE sign on it. It's free because they don't want it or don't need it anymore."

I say nothing.

"Do you even know what I'm talking about?" She turns toward me, green eyes blazing.

"I'm not sure," I say.

"Maybe you'll just decide you don't need me anymore. Maybe you don't really know how to care about anything, really. Except on some kind of *abstract level*." She raises her hands in the air and wiggles her fingers.

"Hold on. We've been traveling together for a couple of months now. We've been in the city for about a week. And we've been together every minute. Do you really think I don't care?"

"Want to know what I think?"

"Yes, I do."

Marianne rises from the bench, turns, and levels a finger at me. "I think you like to keep the world at an arm's length, Ross. Like those eighty-eight keys. And I don't like it one bit."

"You might have noticed that we didn't spend most of last night *at an arm's length*. In fact, we were about as close as two people can be, as far as I can tell."

"Just because you were actually inside me instead of just touching me, doesn't mean we're close," she shouts. Marianne's powerful voice reverberates down Fifth Avenue, freezing pedestrians in their tracks for blocks. They turn and give me withering looks. *What the hell's wrong with that waiter? And what's he doing with that hot chick? Isn't that Julianne Moore?*

They move on. Marianne sits back down.

"Sorry," she says. "I'm emotional."

"So am I, believe it or not."

"I'll believe it when I see it. And not just when you're chan-neling all those dead piano players during a gig."

"It's been a long time since I've been with someone else. You know that."

"Me too, Ross. I'm just saying it's time to forget about all that and let it go. Forget about the stupid ex-boyfriends and -girlfriends. And everyone we met and ripped off on the road. They're not here. They mean nothing now, right?"

I nod. "Nothing."

"So that just leaves the two of us. And a big question."

"What's that?"

"Are you willing to really love someone?"

I jump from the bench. "I don't even know why you're asking this, Marianne. I haven't been with anyone in years. Maybe I'm rusty about saying exactly how I feel. But you've got to know that I'm in love with you, Marianne. Hear that?"

No one walking through the park stops—shouting about love, lost or found, is old news in the city. "I'll even quit stealing."

The people streaming by pause for a moment, then move on. Tough crowd. I sit back down.

"That's not what I'm asking, Ross," she says. "I just want one thing from you."

"What's that?"

"I just want you to trust me. All the time. Not just in bed or on stage or on the road. Just give in and trust me. I'll never do anything to make you regret it."

I pause for a moment. "Of course," I say. "You don't even have to ask."

We kiss, not the tentative kisses of young lovers, but like con-fident pros, who know exactly what they're getting into and where it might lead. Two grifters, off to see the world.

———————

I click on the overhead light. My studio apartment on Elizabeth Street is nearly empty and even more desolate than I remember. A futon. A couple of suitcases full of old clothes. Some books. One window faces a brick wall about five feet away. If I look up at just the right angle, I can see the back of another apartment on Mott Street. Malcolm never claimed that a studio in the clubhouse was elegant, but the price is right. Anyone on the circuit can rent one for five hundred dollars a month.

I sit on the futon for a moment, feel the presence of an earlier self, one more spartan and single-minded. The earlier, more doctrinaire version of me—the felonious monk who lived solo, played the piano, stole, and gave the money away—is dead.

I fold up the futon and drag it down the stairs and out the front door, leaving it on the sidewalk.

Malcolm's merry lodgers share the shadowy main room of the clubhouse. The usual clump of musicians gathers near the old Mason & Hamlin upright, passing charts back and forth, lost in arcane chords and melodies. They look up when I walk in.

"Hey Ross, check this out," someone says. Malcolm's crew knows me as someone who has managed to stay out on the circuit long after most players drop out.

They're huddled around Harry Briggs, a journeyman guitarist who specializes in suburban bank jobs. He's tapping on a laptop.

"You're not going to believe this scam." Harry points at the screen, runs his hand through his long, thinning hair. "You agree to play their set and they cut you a check for five hundred bucks."

The others gathered around the computer scrawl down a phone number in their fakebooks.

"Who are they?"

"Companies. Mostly consumer products. Anyone trying to generate a buzz about their small-batch Bourbon, celebrity fragrance, new car, whatever. You just play the songs they tell you to, work in the product name during the between-song banter, and they pay you. And the best thing about it is, they keep paying for as long as the deal is active. Sometimes it's for years."

I look at the list of songs, find them pretty hokey. "Are you really going to do that?"

"Sure, why not? It's easy money, Ross," Harry says. He leans toward me, whispers, "Easier than holding up bank branch offices with a starter gun."

"It just seems kind of wrong. I mean, trying to get people to buy things."

"That's pretty much what we're doing already, Ross, you know that. They've just broadened the mission a little bit."

"The mission?"

"Yeah, like it says right here." He points—"*Our mission is to expand the unconventional marketing opportunities for innovative products by tapping the talents of America's touring musicians.*"

"I'd rather play *Moondance* until I drop dead."

The others laugh.

Harry smiles. "Choose your poison, friend."

Back upstairs, I haul out my suitcases and put them on the sidewalk. Someone has already dragged off the futon. My years as a boarder in Malcolm's nest of thieves are over.

Malcolm rarely comes to the clubhouse. He prefers a worn Italian restaurant down on Mulberry, where he sits at a café table and drinks espresso in the afternoon, switching to Barolo exactly at five, Scotch at seven.

I join him at his table. He's wearing a narrow-cut Savile Row suit in a delicate pinstripe. His hair is almost completely gray now, swept straight back, making him look like an extremely dapper Charlie Watts.

"Good shows, I hear," he says. His glimmering brown eyes still follow every woman who walks by.

"Definitely." I pick up Malcolm's silver lighter from the table and relight his small cigar.

"Club owners are happy. Lots of return bookings. You're going to be busy this winter."

I pause. "I want to talk to you about something, Malcolm."

"Sure." He drains his glass.

"I'm thinking of switching over to a duo."

Malcolm knocks the ash from his cigar. "Let me guess. You and the talented, lovely Marianne London."

"Yes."

"Well, well," he says, smiling. "Such a surprise."

"I thought you might have been doing some matchmaking." Maybe Malcolm, not fate, brought us together.

He shakes his head. "I can't take credit for it, though I'd be glad to. It just happened. Like everything else in the world. And good for you that it did."

"I think so."

"You don't want to end up like me, Ross. Lonely and too old to do anything about it." Malcolm signals for another glass of wine. "Not that I'm complaining, mind you."

"It's not like we're leaving the circuit," I say. "We want to play out together. Same rooms we're playing now, maybe even bigger."

"How's your chemistry?"

"We played out a few times together and went over great. Been practicing our timing." I think about our long afternoons in the Waldorf Towers.

"I can imagine. And I think you're smart to look for a new angle. Can't keep doing the same thing over and over, Ross. Makes you a very dull boy." Malcolm smiles and the lines in his face deepen for a moment.

"So you think it's a good idea?"

He shrugs. "If it's what you want to do, then it's a good idea."

I try to guess what Malcolm's telling me. For years, he's been my advisor, closer to me than my father, brother, anyone.

"What I'm saying is, if you become a duo, you can't go back, Ross. It's like deciding to play weddings or to put together a band. Once you get your names out there, you have to stick with it, through thick and thin . . . or thin and thinner, more likely."

"Like getting married."

"Like getting married and then some. Take it from me, I've seen plenty of duos go out in my time, and not a lot of them come back."

"What happens?"

"They get tired of each other, burn out, fight about money, drink too much, fool around. There are lots of endings, none of them particularly good."

"Marianne and I are different."

Malcolm's green eyes turn cold for a moment. "That's what everyone thinks."

"We have a lot in common."

"I assume you're not talking about a mutual appreciation for the early stride era."

"I'm talking about extracurricular activities."

"Don't talk too loudly about them." Malcolm leans closer. "Things have been a bit strange lately. I'm like a spider at the center of a web. I feel something new crawling out on the edges of our little nighttime universe. And it isn't good."

"Anything I should look out for?"

"New friends," he says. "Always be worried about new friends. You never know what they can bring. New friends can be enemies you just haven't sized up yet. You're a fast study. You'll be fine. Just keep your eyes open. And your bag packed."

"I will."

"I know you will." He reaches over and squeezes my shoulder. "You're the one the others want to be, Ross. You're legendary."

"Don't you have to be dead to be legendary?"

"Not always, but it helps."

providence

Pale lights glimmer in the low hills that surround downtown.
I'm staring out the window after my second set at the Biltmore
while Marianne takes a bath. Among the earthbound constellations, I see a good life with Marianne—on the road, in New
York, anywhere. Our years together are just starting to unfold.
Ahead we have days of road-tested revelations, nights of learning to hear our secret melodies behind all the standards. It all
looks pretty good to me.

Then the phone rings.

"Where the hell have you been?" Ray is drunk.

"Downstairs. Just played two sets. Good ones, in case you're interested."

"Not where were you tonight, I mean where have you been for the last week."

"New York."

"I tried there. You're usually at the Elysée."

"We stayed at the Waldorf."

"*Whoa.* Going fancy on us, are you?"

"It was great." I remember the slow days high above the city.

"That's good. Because while you were having such a great time, everyone was going nuts looking for you. I e-mailed you. I called Malcolm's clubhouse. And I called all your usual hotels between Baltimore and Boston, you name it."

"Have a sudden need to talk to your little brother?"

"Kind of." He pauses. "Ross, Chief's dead."

I'm suddenly aware of the carpet beneath my feet, of the gravity that draws me to it. "He's in the hospital, you mean. He's sick."

"No, he's dead and buried. He died Monday. The funeral was yesterday. They couldn't wait."

I sit on the bed, lower my head to my knees. I can't imagine Chief dead, can't picture him as anything but my fearless, raven-haired father. He's behind his desk at Moore's Frozen Foods. He's moving up the ladder, building a career, making life better for us. He's shaking the hands of presidents.

"You there?"

The phone has drifted away from my ear and I bring it back. "Yes."

"He's dead, Ross. When I was a kid, I hoped for it. I really did. I wished he would just go die." Ray's voice cracks. "And when he took off for Washington, I *really* wanted him dead."

"That was a long time ago."

"But I never really figured it all out. Never made him proud of me or found a way of dealing with him that didn't make me mad. Now I can't ever do that. I missed my chance."

"When was the last time you saw him?"

"Ten years ago, probably. Back when I could still travel."

"Did you ever tell him what you were doing?"

"Sort of. I made it sound important and on the level. The kind of shit he'd be proud of." Ray can barely speak. It sounds as though someone's hands are tightening around his throat.

"When I saw him in the hospital, he was really proud of you, Ray."

"You got to be kidding." Ray sounds like he's laughing and crying. "I don't think what I'm doing is the kind of making money that Chief had in mind for me. Neither of us are exactly chips off the old block."

Marianne walks in wearing a white bathrobe with the Biltmore logo on the front. She sees tears streaming down my face, then sits on the bed next to me. She puts her hand on my shoulder.

"Ray, I'm really sorry."

"Call Vivian when you get a chance. She was all frantic when we couldn't find you for the funeral. Secretary of Labor was there. Nice obit in the *Times*. They called him an American political success story, and I quote, *rising from a watermelon farm to the upper echelons of Beltway power.*"

"Chief hated growing up on a watermelon farm."

"They didn't say he liked it, bro."

"Did they mention the grand jury investigations?"

"Yeah, they did. It's all part of the package. They described him as a mixed figure. Like anyone in power politics. Anyway, I thought you read the papers every day."

"I've been busy."

"Don't bullshit me. You're knee-deep in pussy. Cray told me all about it."

"Thanks for that."

"All I can say is two words—Chief and Eileen. Remember listening to them screaming at each other in the kitchen every night?"

"Of course. But Ray, that was a long, long time ago. And now they're both dead." Our original audience, the two people we wanted most to impress or shock, is gone. Now we have to figure out who's in the house for our second act.

"Just don't get all normal on me and start settling down, saving up for a house. Shit like that is scary. Really scary."

"And really unlikely."

"It's simple, Ross. When someone as naïve as you falls in love, he's going to get his fingers burned."

"All I can say is I don't think that's going to happen."

"You probably didn't think Chief was going to die, either. Or that Cray was going to get the shit kicked out of him," Ray sputters. "Maybe it's time for you to wake up and spend a little time in reality, Ross. Until then, I don't want to fucking hear from you."

The phone clicks off.

I toss the phone on the bed, stunned. My ears are ringing.

"Bad news from Washington, I assume," Marianne says.

"Yes." I bend forward, close my eyes. "My father's dead."

Marianne puts her arms around me, kisses the back of my neck. "I'm really sorry, Ross."

I say nothing for a few minutes, travel back to when I saw Chief in his hospital room. I can't remember what our final words were, though I'm sure our conversation was as inconclusive and one-sided as usual. "I wasn't a very good son," I say. "And I'm not a particularly good brother or uncle, while we're at it."

"That's not true."

"Trust me, it is."

"You did what you did." Marianne gets up to bring me a Scotch from the minibar. "You can't change it now. It's all in the past."

The first sip from the tiny bottle tastes burnt and bitter. Powerful Chief, distraught Eileen, devious Ray. They're just mythical characters from my childhood, like Miles, Monk, and Bird.

"I bet you remember plenty of stories about your father," Marianne says. "You should tell me some."

"That might take a while." Revisiting the same family episodes over and over leaves them as smooth as old coins, shining brightly though the dates and details are worn away. Everyone carries a handful of familial change.

"We'll stay up as late as you need to. You only get terrible news like this twice in your life."

Marianne brings a blanket into the living room. We kiss, then we sit quietly on the couch, sadness washing over me every few minutes. I spend the rest of the night lost in the past, where so much of my family resides. Time shifts the chords from major to minor to diminished. They're souls swirling above the flatlands, my grandfather, my mother, and now, inconceivably, my father— strong, driven, distant, dead.

In a way, Chief started me down the path to my nightwork. During the summer when I turned sixteen, he got tired of hearing me pound away on the piano and signed me up for a job as a sorter at Moore's Frozen Foods. An internship, he called it, though it was more like an internment. I stood at the side of an enormous stainless steel ramp, wearing a white coat, cap, and plastic gloves, and watched as newly frozen peas bounced down the ramp. My job was to cull the undersized or oversized peas and toss them down a chute. These would be packaged and sold to schools and prisons and other places that didn't care about the uniformity of their peas.

My first day, a training session identified all the rogue elements a sorter might encounter. Rocks, frozen bits of pea tendrils, Band-Aids, pieces of glove, nails, fingernails, mice—all were illustrated in an enormous poster, KNOW YOUR FOREIGN OBJECTS.

I stood at my station for four hours at a time, until my legs ached and my fingertips were half-frozen. I was the youngest of the sorters and vulnerable to pranks. *Playboy* centerfolds, cigarettes, and car keys all found their way down my ramp and I dutifully weeded them out.

Sometimes I'd look up to see Chief in the windowed meeting room above the manufacturing area. He might be sitting at the conference table, smoke rising from his Winston as he berated the middle managers. Or he might be standing at the window, watching me like the God of Frozen Foods.

After a few weeks, I developed new muscles in my shoulders and legs and they quit hurting. My hands were always fast on the keyboard, but now they had a new purpose—to work and make money. I found that the conveyor had a speed control that the plant set automatically to 5. I nudged mine up to 6 and the peas flew even faster. But I could still spot the misshapen ones and the debris, and weed it all out.

Next week, I was up to 8, my hands a blur over the ever-advancing green peas.

At *9,* my eyes could never leave the conveyor, just pinball back and forth. My hands darted out like a cat's paws. A cat on meth. Line workers on break gathered around me, shaking their heads, sure I couldn't keep it up shift after shift. But I did. Above, Chief beamed, pointed me out to his colleagues. His boy was no workplace flyweight.

When I moved the setting to *10,* pea sorting entered a whole new level, one that even Cray and his Japanese gamer friends would find interesting. I had to hunch over the bouncing peas, making multiple catches with one hand, lunging for the occasional rock. A crowd gathered every time I stepped up to the sorter. I was featured in Moore's newsletter, *The Flash*—a nod to the flash-frozen process.

Then Moore's fired me. Or "reallocated" me to the shipping room, tracking outgoing shipments with the help of an enormous beige computer. Chief explained that the other sorters complained, and my fast work was creating chaos in the packaging department. I had discovered that my fast hands could help me make a living, attract attention, and get me into trouble.

boston

By the end of the first set at the Copley Plaza, my fingers ache and sweat pours down my face. It's an easy crowd, but I play it hard, hovering over the keyboard, rising up slightly from the bench, head nodding. I think of James P. Johnson playing four hours straight at the Pied Piper Club and Bud Powell's breakneck runs during the Clef sessions. By the end the crowd is on its feet cheering me on like I'm running the Boston Marathon. But the show isn't for them. I'm trying to outrun the inevitable slowing of my ten fingers. I'm postponing the final set of the ultimate gig, the one that involves keeling over on the floor and dying. Fear is pushing me on, leaving the keys hot and sweat-slick and my mind racing.

"What the hell was going on out there?" Marianne rubs my shoulders in our suite between sets.

"Just wanted to show them what I can do."

"Pace yourself, there's another set in ten minutes. They pay the same no matter how many notes you play. And people who are eating dinner don't like to see the pianist spraying sweat like a rock star."

I nod. While Marianne finishes dressing, I walk to the window and look out at tidy Back Bay with its frost-tilted brick sidewalks and million-dollar brownstones. Boston looks elegant and worn tonight, like the striped Brooks Brothers shirts Chief favored.

After the Boston shows, we'll go back to New York and work up a new set. Malcolm is already planning our first tour as a duo.

Marianne comes out wearing her favorite dark blue silk dress. "We better get back downstairs." She kisses me on the lips and then pushes away to look straight into my eyes. "Let's make this the last night," she says.

"What do you mean?"

"Let's make this the last night we pick up strangers and rob them."

I say nothing. We leave the amber glow of the suite and walk hand in hand down the long narrow hall toward the elevators.

"You're ready to give it up. You told me yourself," Marianne says. "And God knows I'm not craving another night with an old man with a thick wallet and an ass wattle."

"I don't have either of those."

"Thank God."

"What will you do for extra money, you know, to pay your mother's bills?"

She shrugs. "I'll figure out something. Malcolm can get us holiday gigs, book us on a long tour. Cruise ships! Or maybe we can play in Germany—resort hotels pay crazy money."

We get in the elevator. "You're saying you want to go completely straight?" I ask.

"I'm saying I just want to be with you," Marianne says.

"That sounds really good." I lean forward and kiss her. We stay locked together until the elevator bell dings and the door opens.

The lobby is airless and full of people. A celebrity fundraiser in the main ballroom just let out and most of the crowd is heading toward the bar. Every seat is already full. The manager waves us through the door, jabs his finger toward the stage. "Go start your set."

"Any requests?"

"Just play until I tell you to stop," he shouts.

Marianne takes the microphone from the stand, cradles it for a moment until it begins to crackle, then drops down almost to her knees to hit the first note of *I've Got You Under My Skin,* delivered with half-closed eyes. The crowd pushes toward us, drawn away from the bar and toward the stage where we play a set that defies hotel bar rules. Marianne doesn't talk up the crowd. There are no lulls that let drunk men lurch up to the tip jar. No time for people to talk and buy more drinks. Every moment is filled with music—long, frenetic solos from me, chorus after chorus from Marianne. *Devil May Care, Let's Fall in Love*—the set races along. People are standing ten deep in the back, dancing between the tables. Waitresses stumble. Glasses smash.

Sweat-blinded and floating somewhere high above the Steinway, I'm hammering the spinet back in my father's living room. I'm playing Malcolm's old Club Solano in Chicago. I'm playing every hotel bar in the country. I'm pounding out every song I know all at once. We're lost in the stars, high over the old devil moon, the summer wind taking us to the east of the sun.

Manic applause greets our marathon set. We close with *The Man I Love* and Marianne strides back and forth along the edge of the low stage, stepping into the audience. I know she's not looking for another man to love, just one last man to rob. A slower song lets me check out the tables more closely and I find them rife with possibilities, necklaces glimmering in the candlelight, engagement rings, even tiaras. *Who the hell wears a tiara?* I smile, draw their owners toward me with whatever charm I have left.

In the back of the room there's a serious man in a suit, surrounded by a posse of younger guys. I can't place his face for a minute, then I remember the Banana Man lying in a king-sized bed wearing nothing but a yellow condom and a drug smile.

Marianne stands at the microphone, scans the crowd for men with gray hair, an eager gaze, and solid-gold credit.

I work in a two-bar tease, a wisp of melody from *Day-O* by Harry Belafonte. Miles managed to work *Skip to My Lou* into *Sid's Ahead* and *Jeeper's Creepers* into *Little Melonae*. My tease is a warning. I'm hoping that Marianne will remember the next line—*Come Mr. Tally Man, tally me banana.*

She just turns and gives me a confused look.

We finish the set and the crowd stands up and applauds.

Marianne smiles, walks over to the piano and points to me graciously. "What the hell was that?" she whispers during the applause.

"Banana Man's out there."

"No way."

"Saw him in the back. Maybe he's come back for more."

"All the way from Philadelphia for a handjob? I don't think so."

"Like moths to a flame."

"I'm no flame, Ross." Marianne takes one last bow. "And believe me, that guy was no moth."

"Good." I look back to the third table from the front, searching for a dark-haired woman with a gleaming necklace, the one begging *steal me*.

We climb the wide stone stairs of the town house, my last diamond donor and I. Roxanne fumbles for her keys and bends toward me suddenly, kissing me half on the mouth, half on my chin. Her lips are slick and hard as orange rind. Inside, we pass through an entryway lined with framed portraits. Mixed in among the scowling men are factories, lovingly framed and annotated at the bottom—Cleveland, Santa Ana, Minneapolis.

"Those are Ned's," she says in passing, pulling me up the stairs by my hand. "His family's from Scotland originally, like a way long time ago. He has a thing for genealogy. These are his relatives."

"He has buildings for relatives?"

"No, those are his factories, silly. He makes adhesive office products—labels, file folder tags, things like that. He sold his company to a bigger one in Hong Kong. Now he just lectures about how to run a business. You've probably seen him on television. The Scottish tape baron . . ."

I nod, recognize the demi-business celebrity that is Ned McLeish, a scrappy seventy-something industrialist with a bad temper. *Nuclear Ned,* articles called him. His current wife seems to be about thirty years younger than him, though it's hard to say. Away from the low light of the hotel bar, Roxanne is looking heavily renovated.

Roxanne 2.0 leads me on, past a spotless kitchen big as a restaurant's, then up the slow spiral of the staircase, lined with portraits of more cruel-looking people. They scowl, wonder what a lowlander musician/jewel thief is doing here in the hallowed fallout shelter of Nuclear Ned.

We pass a room full of workout equipment, CNN blaring from a wall-sized flatscreen, followed by an enormous office with two Mission-style desks facing each other, both empty.

The third-floor bedroom looks out over Beacon Hill and across the Charles River to Cambridge. Roxanne goes to her bureau and takes off the enormous necklace that first attracted me to her, a heavy piece more Los Angeles than Boston. She places it carefully in a gray clamshell box.

When he's not yelling at people or out on the lecture circuit, apparently Ned is buying diamonds. There's a five-carat cushion-cut platinum engagement ring, the two-carat diamond drops, and whatever other loot waits in Roxanne's top drawer. I unzip Roxanne's gown and she steps out of it casually, revealing perfectly tanned legs, black French-cut panties, and an aerodynamic bra.

Roxanne strides into the bathroom and opens the medicine cabinet.

She points at the pharmacopia crowding the shelves. "Most of these are Ned's. He's got a lot of things starting to go wrong."

Now he has another. A musician is running his hands up his wife's spine, perhaps the only area of her body that hasn't been visited by the knives and lasers of modern flesh sculptors.

"Wait a second," she says as she peers into the medicine cabinet. "I really want to enjoy this." She thoughtfully fingers one amber prescription bottle after another.

"You will, I promise," I say.

"But if I take one of these and two of these." She pops the bottles off the shelves, opening one after the next, tossing back the bright pills without water. "Then I can be sure."

Roxanne guides me into the bedroom and sprawls across the white cotton duvet cover. "Make me scream, Rob."

"Ross," I say quietly, then start rubbing her ankles just like I have so many others, so many times. Hands have no allegiance. They are just tools of my trade, no different from calipers. My fingers explore Roxanne's tight leg, moving quickly, the way they do when rushing to finish a request. That's what I'm trying to do with Roxanne—finish. I hope Marianne has performed her last creditectomy and is waiting back in our suite at the Copley.

Roxanne murmurs for a moment, then goes silent. It's like massaging the dead.

When I first started my nightwork, I was convinced that everyone could be awakened and brought back to their senses. But here at the end, I'm not convinced that it's possible, or right for me to try.

After half an hour, I reach up and poke Roxanne's leg, get no response, then poke harder.

Roxanne's skin feels really strange. I lean closer and squint. I pinch her skin and lift a little. She's wearing a layer of some kind of elastic microfiber, tight as an extra skin, one without blemishes, veins, ambitious hairs. An almost-undetectable zipper runs from under her arms to her knees. I open it and let Roxanne's real body out, a half-size larger now.

Her false skin is light as ash, custom-made and expensive, no doubt. I wad it up into a ball no bigger than a fist, open the window, and toss Roxanne out. Her skin hovers for a moment, as if unable to leave its owner, then billows out over Beacon Hill, swooping down Charles Street like a soul looking for a new body.

I walk to the bed, check to make sure Roxanne is still breathing. She is, and I suppose that's good, though I'm not so sure. She's on her way from trophy to atrophy and nothing I can do will slow her passage.

In the bedroom mirror, my eyes are red, body pale—a night creature on a final hunt. I pull my magnifier from my fakebook and survey one last jewelry drawer, looking for clarity and brilliance.

Anyone awake in Boston at two in the morning is probably up to no good, myself included. The moon is nearly full, turning the Common into a black-and-white dreamscape. Next to a fountain, I see the orange glow of a cigarette burning in the shadows beneath a green blanket. Another man lies along a bench, eyes closed, copper skin shining in the moonlight. I take out a stack of hundreds and peel off two, tucking them into his parka.

By the time I get near Copley Square, my fakebook is emptied of cash, delivered to night-sleepers and park-sprawlers. I scoop out the hoard of diamonds I've stolen from Roxanne, then, after a long pause, drop my fakebook in a trash can.

We're heading into a new era, Marianne and I, and this moon-lit night seems like the right time to get rid of old routines. I don't need Delmar's fakebook anymore. I never look at the charts and melodies. They're always with me, coded into my hands by finger memory.

The battered fakebook looks little different from the rest of the trash nestled in among the crushed paper bags and newspapers. I put one of the diamonds, a carat or so, on top of the book, and it glimmers among the debris, moonlight ricocheting through the facets and back out again. It's beautiful.

I walk on, past stores and churches, all closed now. The first leaves have already fallen and they crackle beneath my shoes. The sun will be rising soon and early commuters will start to gush from the trolley stops. Men in tan raincoats and blue blaz-ers will march up Boylston Street, heading to their jobs.

An old man with a thick gray beard is curled on a red blanket in front of Trinity Church, an overcoat wrapped around him. I read the careful handwriting on his cardboard sign. TOO PROUD TO BEG, TOO HONEST TO STEAL—wisdom from the mouths of bums.

Something shifts in my mind. Despite all my excuses, I'm not too honest to steal. I may be a generous thief, but I'm still a thief.

I drop the diamonds into his paper cup and keep walking.

Marianne is watching a movie in our suite at the Copley, a thriller with lots of shouting. She must be having trouble sleep-ing, or maybe she's just waiting up for me to celebrate the end of our nightwork. I open the door, glad to be home, ready for our thieving days to be over.

All the lights are on. Marianne sits in a straight-back chair in the center of the living room, her arms and legs tied with bath-robe belts.

Two men in black suits grab me from both sides, lift me off the floor, and carry me into the living room.

"Ross, I'm sorry, I . . ."

"Shut the fuck up, songbird." Banana Man rises from the couch and clicks off the television. He gives me a sick smile. His cohorts dump me in a chair.

"Back so soon? Enjoying a little Boston nightlife?"

I nod.

"Then you're a lying sack of shit, because there is no Boston nightlife. They roll the carpets up at midnight and it's . . ."

One of the Banana Man's thugs checks his watch, then puts his sleeve back in place. "Almost three in the morning."

"*In the wee, wee hours of the morning, when the world is fast asleep.* Isn't that the Sinatra line?"

"I hate Frank Sinatra," I say.

"But you weren't counting sheep, were you, piano man? You were counting diamonds. At least that's what your girlfriend said you were doing. After a little coercion. Let's see if you got lucky."

The guys in suits rush forward to pull off my jacket, turn it inside out on the carpet, rip the pockets. They reach their hands into my pants pockets.

"He's got nothing," one of the thugs says.

"Shame, because a few diamonds might be a nice down pay-ment."

"For what?" Marianne says.

"We've been talking about this for hours," Banana Man says. "Don't you remember anything I told you?" His face turns red and his lips stretch away from his mouth, spraying spit.

Marianne says nothing.

"You owe me. And not just a little. My wife tried to charge some dresses at Saks and what happened? Her card was declined. I was at dinner at the Four Seasons and shockingly, my card was declined too, embarrassing me in front of some clients."

Banana Man stalks through the living room in a figure eight that takes him past Marianne, over to the window, then back toward my chair. On the side table next to me is an enormous fruit basket. Next to it waits a gleaming silver fruit knife.

"My accountants looked into it, and found a new Cal Ruderman living in Los Angeles, running up piles of debt, buying cars, and generally being a freeloader. His spending spree came to an untimely end that I won't bother telling you about. It's not good to know the ending of a story too soon."

The thugs laugh, his audience of two.

"Needless to say, this whole incident was not only embarrassing for us," Banana Man says. "It was also a surprise. And I hate surprises."

One of the thugs pipes in. "He does. He really does."

Banana Man walks over to the fruit basket and takes out a bunch of small red bananas. "Take these bananas, for instance. They're from Colombia, right in the heart of drug country. I pay a right-wing death squad, the United Self-Defense Forces of Colombia, plus the Revolutionary Armed Forces, to protect our fields and shoot anyone fucking up our fruit. Costs me about seven million dollars a year. But it's worth it. Because come harvest time, American Fruit doesn't want any surprises. We want bananas."

He tosses the bananas on my lap. "You'll like these, by the way. Really sweet, different from the Mexican crap we unload on Safeway. They're organic. At least that's what we tell people so they can pay more."

The thugs laugh.

"Speaking of delicious fruit . . ." When he passes Marianne, Banana Man nonchalantly reaches down her dress and squeezes her breast, hard.

"Hey!" I shout.

She twists away from him.

"Don't worry. I'm not going to fuck you," he says. "If I wanted to, I would, but I'm not interested in that. That would be too easy. I could just fuck you, then kill you and dump you in one of our container ships. But I want to give you two a little gift that keeps on giving."

The thugs come closer to me.

"Cut off his finger," Banana Man says, as if he's asking for a match.

The thugs throw me into a chair. One pushes my hand down on the side table. The other takes the fruit knife and presses it down on my ring finger at the first joint.

"No!" Marianne struggles in her chair, almost knocking it over.

Banana Man turns to her. "So you don't want your friend here to lose his finger, do you? Because all I have to do is tell them to keep going and it'll be rolling on the carpet, songbird."

"*No,*" she shouts. "I'll give you whatever you want. It's all my fault."

"That's right. But my dad always told me never to hit girls."

Banana Man nods and the thug presses the knife down harder, sending pain shooting up my arm. Blood trickles across the table and drips down into the carpet. I close my eyes.

"*No!*" Marianne screams.

"All your fault, what?"

"All my fault that I sold your information."

"How much did you get for it?"

"Five hundred dollars."

"That's all my identity is worth? Five hundred dollars?"

Marianne shrugs. "No offense, but that's what black Amex cards go for now."

"Well here's my offer, songbird. I want *five million dollars*. In cash. On Friday at two in the afternoon. Or I'll come back and take your boyfriend's finger."

"Five million dollars?" I shout. "Are you crazy?"

"Crazy? Maybe. But what I really am is completely fucking pissed off." Banana Man sprays spit again. "Five million dollars in cash. And no bullshit. Deal?"

The air hums with threat.

"Yes," Marianne says.

The thugs back away and I grab my bleeding hand.

"Now I know what you're thinking, a couple of fast ones like you." Banana Man points to Marianne, then me. "You're looking for the angle. Some way to get out of this jam. Maybe you're thinking about calling my wife and telling her, hoping it will screw the deal. But believe me, she knows about this whole situation. And she thinks five million dollars should just about cover her pain and suffering."

We say nothing.

"Or maybe you're thinking about running. Heading up to Canada or something." He shakes his head. "Not worth it. Eventually you'll surface, and when you do, the deal will be off. By that time, I'll want to cut off more than your finger, piano man." He points at me, smiles.

The thugs laugh.

"So what you're going to do is this. You're going to get in touch with your crooked friends and get them to give you the money. Then you give it to me on Friday at two in the afternoon. Right here in this room. Just us. It's simple. Crooked little fish like you always know some crooked big fish. It's the trickle-up theory."

They drift out of the living room. Banana Man turns at the door and smiles. "Enjoy your fruit basket."

The door clicks closed and I rush to Marianne's chair and untie her.

"What the hell was that?"

"Payback," she says, rubbing her wrists. "You okay?"

"I'm fine." There's a clot the size of a nickel around the cut and a thick streak of blood runs down my palm.

Marianne leads me into the bathroom. "Run it under warm water."

The water pinks up for a moment, then runs clear. I see the cut, a darker line at the first knuckle, as if to mark where to cut on Friday.

"It's just a little cut," I say. "We have bigger problems." I shut off the water and Marianne wraps my hand in a towel.

Back in the living room, Marianne goes to the minibar and takes out two Scotches, twists the tops off, and sets them on the table between us. We sit in hotel chairs.

"Cheers," she says, tipping hers back like a tiny trumpet.

"Did they hurt you?"

"He slapped me around for a while, then got bored. He told

me he was going to let his boys screw me, but I kicked the first one in the balls and started screaming. That's when they tied me up. And you walked in."

"I had no idea he was such a bastard."

"Neither did I." She shakes her head. "I guess that's what it takes to get ahead in the fruit business." She frowns. "I mean, I've been doing this for years. And I'm sure more than a couple of guys figured out where their credit info got stolen. But even if they did, they just paid the fees, changed their credit cards, and moved on."

"Well, I think Cal Ruderman is one of the craziest people I've ever seen. And I've been around a lot of them."

"Crazy and violent. Did you see his eyes?"

I nod. "Ice blue and dead, like cheap sapphires."

"You would think that."

I finish my Scotch, toss the plastic bottle into the fake fireplace. "Not diamonds. He's definitely semi-precious."

"Or semi-psychotic. How does a guy like that run a giant corporation?"

"Really well."

We pause, thinking about what's really on our minds. And it isn't Cal Ruderman's managerial style.

"Where are we going to come up with five million dollars?" I ask.

"I have absolutely no idea." Marianne shakes her head. "I've got a couple hundred thousand in the bank. How about you?"

I shrug. "Less. Lots less."

"Oh yeah," she says. "You've been giving to the poor. Don't you wish you had all that money now?"

"No, not really."

Marianne pulls away, walks to the minibar for another round.

"Are you kidding? You don't wish you just had five million in cash to hand over? It's your finger he's coming back for."

"We're not giving him anything," I say.

"Really, is that what you think?"

"Now it is. At the end of the week, maybe I'll think differently."

Marianne sits next to me, hands me another whiskey. "Well, I think we should call Malcolm first thing in the morning."

"That's exactly what he wants us to do."

"What do you mean?"

"I mean this whole thing could just be a setup. A way to lead someone to Malcolm—he warned me something might be going on. We have to be very, very careful, Marianne." I remembered what Malcolm said about watching out for new friends. Cal Ruderman was no friend, but he was new, and deeply evil.

"What'd you tell him?"

"I sang like a songbird, Ross. They told me they'd kill you if I didn't."

"I don't blame you," I say. "I would have done the same thing."

"What are we going to do now?" Marianne moves closer to me in the chair.

"Sleep. For a little bit, at least. Then we need to come up with a plan."

"Any ideas?"

"We'll make something up. We're good at winging it."

"We'd better be. I like your hands the way they are."

"I do too."

When I first met Malcolm, we sat at his rooftop bar above Solano, a tapas place that switched over to a club at sundown. It was hot and windy, and when he lifted up his vodka tonic the napkin blew into the air. Without looking at it, I caught the napkin between my fingers.

He laughed. "Very lucky." He asked the waiter for a stack of bar napkins and released them one by one like little paper pigeons. Each time, I reached out and trapped the paper between my fingers before the napkin blew down onto the street.

Malcolm smiled. "Remarkable."

"Always been good with my hands." I remembered the steel conveyor belt bouncing with frozen peas.

"It's a gift," Malcolm said. "And like any gift, you need to do something with it."

"I'm playing a lot of gigs at school. I'm not sure what else I could do with it."

"Your brother dragged me along to that basement place."

"The Michigan Tap."

"Right. You're good. Very good. But we have to get you out of the college bars. I'm absolutely sure I could get you some real gigs. And not just in Chicago. How'd you like to go to New York?"

"That'd be great. But I'm in school."

"What would you say if I said I could show you a way to make lots of money?"

I was interested, very interested, but didn't want to be too eager. So I said nothing. Ray had told me to meet with his friend Malcolm, who was "always coming up with ideas."

"You know what the name of my club means?"

I shook my head.

"Solano is what the Spanish call the eastward wind blowing through the Strait of Gibraltar. It's also called the Levanter, as in *toward the soleil levant.*"

I nodded at Malcolm, tried to look like I knew what he was talking about.

"What I'm saying is that sometimes you just have to let the wind carry you, to see where it takes you. Even if it seems . . . off course at first."

"Like heading east to New York."

"Yes, like that. Toward the rising sun." Malcolm leaned forward. "Studying with that Strauss crowd would leave you soulless, Ross. And lead you directly to Washington and into the arms of Reagan and his ilk. I think I could chart a very different course for you. Interested?"

"Yes, of course." I wanted nothing to do with Washington. It was Chief's turf. Plus, it was the last year of Reagan and everyone was sick of him.

"Take this." Malcolm looked both ways to make sure we were alone on the rooftop, then plucked an envelope from the inner pocket of his suit and handed it to me.

"What's in it?"

"Four diamond rings. Good ones. But they have a problem."

"What's that?"

"They're engraved with the names of their previous owners, which poses a little issue in the aftermarket. So I need to have the diamonds removed from their settings with this." He took what appeared to be a set of crossed tweezers from his pocket.

"What are those?"

"Reverse calipers. They remove diamonds. Well, actually, you do the removing. They're just a tool. But kind of hard to use." He handed the calipers to me like a surgeon handing a scalpel to a colleague.

"Take them. Go into the bathroom. And bring me the diamonds." He looked at his Rolex.

I held the envelope in one hand, the calipers in the other, looking back and forth. "But I don't know how." It was like someone asking me to play the xylophone.

Malcolm waved his hand at me, took a sip of his drink. "It's an audition, Ross. You'll figure it out. Go, clock's running."

"I was back in thirty-six seconds," I whisper into the pay phone near the Common. "Remember?"

"Of course. It's a record that still stands." Malcolm's voice sounds thin, far away.

"That seems like a long time ago," I say.

"It was. Thousands of gigs under the bridge."

A pause. I watch people coming out of the Park Street T stop and click open their umbrellas. A light rain glistens the street.

"I don't want to lose my finger, Malcolm. I really don't," I say suddenly.

"I know, Ross. Believe me, if there was an easy way out, we would have come up with it. I just can't get my hands on five million dollars in a few days. Things are very, very bad right now. Credit crunch and all that. In fact, I think you may be right about this being a setup. I wouldn't be surprised if that banana fellow comes back with the feds in tow. Be sure you have nothing on you of any . . . value."

"Believe me, I don't."

"Then we have nothing to worry about."

"But Marianne told them about . . ."

"A confession while getting slapped around? I'm sure that will get thrown out of court. You'll have to take your chances, of course. And they have Marianne on the hook for taking the Banana guy's credit info. But that's not exactly a ticket to jail anymore."

I haven't slept and my head is spinning. Is the Banana Man who he says he is? Are we just being used as bait to catch the bigger fish?

"Ross?"

"Still here."

"Look at the bright side," Malcolm says. "The feds may hold you for a few days. But they're definitely not going to cut off your finger."

"I've got to get back to the hotel room," I say. "Marianne's probably wondering where I am."

"Look, Ross. You're the best player on the circuit. And I'm not talking about the piano. You'll figure the angles out. You're fast."

"I'm not feeling particularly fast right now."

"Give it a day or so. You and Marianne have a three-night stand at the Copley Plaza to distract you."

I shut my eyes. "I almost forgot."

"Well, don't. Just stay cool and play the gig straight. Like you always do. You'll come up with something."

I hang up, walk back across the Common to check the trash can where I left my fakebook. It's gone. No diamonds wait in the dirt. On the stairs of Trinity Church, a new bum sits with his paper cup. I stuff in a Jackson and walk on.

Marianne sits in her bathrobe, tapping away on her laptop, room service tray on the floor next to her. I tell her about my conversation with Malcolm and she throws a coffee cup across the room.

"After all we've given him over the years? If anyone could

scrape up five million dollars, it's Malcolm. A million just isn't what it used to be. He's turned into a paranoid old man, Ross."

"He's being cautious."

"Cautious is going to lose you a finger. We need to be completely bold right now."

"That sounds like something Cray would say."

"Probably."

I nod toward the computer. "What are you doing?"

"Putting out feelers. Seeing if one of my fans admires me enough to cough up five million."

I clear the newspapers and clothes off the couch and sit down. "And?"

"We'll see. It's still early out west. I asked the question. They'll answer it."

"What do you think?"

"Times are tough for the ultra-rich. But I think some romantic or delusional admirer will help out." Marianne walks over to the couch and lies down with her head on my shoulder.

"That feels good."

"Can we forget about Banana Man for a little bit?"

"Yes. But he's not going away."

"I know." Marianne takes my hand in hers, rubs my palm, my fingers, then stops. She starts to cry and I pull her close. "I'm really scared, Ross. I know I'm always acting like I have the admirers in the palm of my hand. But Cal Ruderman is different, like some kind of an intraspecies predator."

"That's an interesting way to describe him."

"I read it in a magazine article about sociopaths. They tend to do very well in business."

"I bet."

She brightens. "I have an idea. We could just get a gun and shoot him when he comes back."

"Shoot him? Just shoot him, like in the head? And the other guys too?" I make a gun with my thumb and index finger.

"Yeah, like that."

"Then dump them into a hole somewhere and escape into the Florida sunset?"

"Sounds good."

"We're not in a crime novel, Marianne," I say. "It's just not that easy."

During our gig, I scan the crowd for diamonds. Old habits die hard.

It's a fund-raiser for a hospital and the crowd is filled with rich donors and their wives. More jewels than ever taunt me. I just stare at them like an alcoholic at a wine shop.

Once diamonds meant late-night hotel room stealth. They meant excitement. I was powerless before them. I had to steal them. But now they hold no allure at all.

They might as well be black opals from the playground.

We launch into *The Man I Love,* the song where Marianne usually sends her patented hooked gaze out into the shimmering crowd, trolling for men willing to trade unhappiness for adventure—and a shot credit rating. Instead of looking out into the crowd, she stays in the curve of the piano, turns her gaze on me. She smiles.

We used to play our gigs like we were simply a singer and accompanist. Staying aloof gave the audience someone to be attracted to, a focus for their desire. It's the first law of duos. Do not act like you're in love. No one wants to see other people in love, Malcolm told me once. It's like being hungry and watching someone else eat a steak.

But during this set, it's becoming clear to everyone that we're not strangers. Not at all. We're looking at each other as if we're back in the Waldorf, preparing for a second reading of the collected works of Conrad Hilton.

The tip jar can stays empty. People can complain. We don't care. We're in love. And also in big trouble.

I lie in bed and watch the lights from the street flicker on the ceiling, like television without the people or places. Ceiling TV always soothes me in strange hotels, alone or with a sleeping diamond donor. But tonight it does little to slow my racing mind. I think of all the angles that will help me avoid Banana Man's knife.

We've ruled out killing him.

We did the math and realized that a desperate three-day thievery binge wouldn't net us more than a million in diamonds, BMWs, and credit.

Malcolm is no help at all.

A new plan stretches out like a young vine, but I'm not sure whether it's the right approach or just the only one that seems possible. From years of improvising, I know that the first impulse is always too close to the melody, that it's best to skip it and look further afield.

Marianne stirs. "You're awake, aren't you?"

"Yes."

She presses against me, kisses my neck. "I feel terrible."

"Why?"

"The admirers."

Marianne's pleas for cash came back with rejections, polite and otherwise. "Did you really think some sucker would come up with five million dollars?" I ask.

"No, but I thought five of them would come up with a million each."

"Why should they?"

"They like me?"

"People can like you and not want to give you any of their money. Most men want nothing more than to hang on to their money. It's everything to them. Their barometer of happiness. Suicides skyrocket when the market takes a big drop."

"Thanks for the Wolfshead Boys sermon. It's not helpful to get all preachy."

"I'm just saying that asking your admirers for a million dollars is different than them buying you a nice dinner or giving you a necklace. More expensive, more risky."

"Everything's risky. Walking down the street, living, falling in love."

Marianne kisses me and soon we're floating on love's warm, shallow pond again. I reach for her. She urges me inside and we rise and fall, sink and surface, swim toward the sun.

"So that's your best plan? That's how you're going to save us?" Marianne half-rises from our booth and I reach out to stop her. The other people in the diner look up at our lover's squabble.

I smile to reassure them, and Marianne, that everything's fine.

She settles back down, but tentatively.

"I'm not saying it's going to work." My voice is low and urgent. Night after night of not sleeping has left me jittery. "I just think it's worth a try."

"You can't negotiate with a psychopath, Ross."

"You can negotiate with anyone."

"No. Your father could negotiate with anyone. You can play the piano. And steal."

"That's what you think I am, then?" I say. "A piano player and a thief?"

"Calm down, Ross. This isn't about what I think of you. Why don't you call your brother the counterfeiter and just ask him for five million in his handiwork?"

I lean forward, look around the diner. "Could you not shout? Ray doesn't do hundreds. He does twenties. And in limited amounts. He doesn't have anything near five million in cash. Ask Cray."

"I just might. Because I want to get through this whole mess with all your fingers intact."

"And without him hurting you, either. I don't want him to touch you again."

"What will you do, Ross? *Negotiate with him* until he agrees to quit being a psychopath?"

I think of my father's saying about the Wolfshead Boys—*one weak, one weird*. I always considered myself the weird one but now I'm not so sure.

"I'll think of something," I say.

"You'd better do it fast, he's coming back tomorrow. And we don't have our act together. Not at all. It's amateur hour all the way. We have to try everything. I mean everything—beg, borrow, or steal!" Marianne knocks over a coffee cup as she stands up. The Cambridge hipsters in the diner peer at us through designer eyewear as Marianne pulls on her raincoat and rushes out into Davis Square. I follow her to the door, then go back to our booth to think, worry, pay the bill.

Several cups of coffee later, I remember what Chief told me in the hospital. At the time, his advice seemed morphine-clouded. But now it makes more sense. I can remember lyrics to hundreds of songs, but I can't remember my father's exact words. *Negotiating is about how much you're willing to give up.* That's how I remember it. Thinking about Banana Man, I know that I'm willing to give up a lot to stay with Marianne and keep her safe.

Despite what I told Marianne, I know I can't negotiate with Banana Man, try to work out some kind of payment plan, or try to convince him to take less money. He wants to leave with something. A promise isn't enough. I'm willing to give him what he's asking for so I get what I want—the rest of my life with Marianne.

Even if that means losing my finger.

"He's late, the motherfucker."

"I'm not exactly in a hurry to see him," I say. It's past two-thirty on Friday and Marianne and I are pacing around our suite as if it's a hospital waiting room.

"Let's leave." Marianne grabs both my hands. "Come on, now."

I shake my head. "He'll find us."

"No he won't. This whole thing may be a setup, like you said."

At three o'clock, there's a hard knock on the door. I answer it and in strut Banana Man and his two sidekicks. They look like they did during their last visit, well-dressed and evil.

"Greetings." Banana Man reaches out to shake but I don't put out my hand.

He gives a big bleached-teeth smile. "Afraid I might just go ahead and pull that finger off, are you?"

The goons, his weaselly audience, laugh.

Banana Man turns serious. "Well, I will if I don't get what I came for."

"Why do you want five million dollars?" I ask. "The whole identity theft thing cost you a couple thousand at most."

Banana Man walks to the center of the room as if he's about to address an auditorium full of shareholders. He lifts his face to speak to the ceiling. "It's about pain and suffering."

"You think you experienced significant pain and suffering because your credit rating dropped momentarily? Because you had to hire someone to fix it?"

Banana Man locks his gaze on me and his blue eyes narrow. "You don't have the money, do you? Is that what you're saying?"

I hold my hand in the air, palm forward. "Just bear with me for a moment, then you can cut off my finger. I just want to get something straight first."

Banana Man looks at his Rolex. "You got exactly one minute, and then we'll go over there to that table and finish the job."

Marianne is pacing around the room, palms pressing over her ears, as if she can block out what's about to happen. "Jesus, Ross," she hisses. "Do something."

"I just think you should consider the numbers," I say.

Banana Man smiles. "Oh yeah? I already have. I'm getting five million in cash in exchange for letting you keep your finger."

"Exactly! That's the problem," I say. "You run a big company. A market leader. So you know that our whole economy, our model of democracy even, is based on free markets."

Banana Man nods. "Of course. Free markets fucking rule."

"And that means that commodities, like fruit . . ." I pick up an apple from the fruit basket. "Are worth what people are willing to pay for them."

"Not to interrupt, but did you try those little bananas?"

"You know, I did," I say. "And I have to tell you, they were really, really good."

Banana Man turns to his handlers. "Told you he'd eat them." He turns back to me. "Sorry, we had a little side bet going."

"For what, the five million?"

"Of course not, for twenty bucks."

I point at Banana Man's chest. "Exactly my point. That bet isn't worth five million dollars. So you set a value on it—twenty dollars, which seemed reasonable."

"So what?"

"Sometimes commodities get wildly overvalued. Tulip bulbs in Holland in the 1700s, for example. Nutmeg in the colonial era. More recently—mortgage-backed securities. In any case, overpricing these commodities always ends badly, with a massive market correction and lots of turmoil."

Banana Man looks at his watch. "You're talking out your ass, aren't you? Get to your point. Then we'll get to ours." One of his goons takes out a box cutter and pushes the blade out with his thumb.

I'm winging it, improvising, postponing the inevitable. Totally out of ideas, I borrow from anything and everything, pulling out all the stops. "My point is that my finger isn't worth five million dollars. By insisting that it is, you're putting it all at risk—our economy, democracy, freedom."

Banana Man's eyes open wide and he exhales loudly. "What the fuck! What we do in this room isn't going to affect anything except your ability to play the piano. Just shut the fuck up and go put your hand on that table. Like a man. Or we'll drag you over there screaming and kicking like a little sissy."

"I'm just saying that it's all connected, micro and macro, overpriced little bananas and . . ."

"Those bananas are priced fairly," he shouts, face red.

"But this . . ." I wiggle the finger that Banana Man wants to remove. "Is one overpriced finger. Way overpriced. There are millions of fingers." I walk over to the table and put my hand firmly on the wood, palm down. "If you really want to cut it off, go ahead. But it's a big mistake on a lot of levels—economic, moral, criminal . . ."

There's a loud knock. Everyone freezes and turns toward the door.

"Expecting someone?" Banana Man asks. Guns materialize in the goons' hands.

"Room service," a voice says.

Marianne strides toward the door. "I ordered champagne to celebrate."

Banana Man blocks her way. "To celebrate what?"

"The arrival of your five million in cash," she says, stepping past him. "And your imminent departure."

Before Banana Man can stop her, Marianne throws open the door.

The goons put their guns away and take a sudden interest in the view of Copley Square on a rainy afternoon. I raise my hand from the side table.

A room service guy in a blue uniform and bow tie pushes a white cart into the room. He takes the champagne from a silver cooler of ice, deftly removes the metal cage, and twists off the cork with a dull pop. He pours the flutes full, then hands Marianne the small leather binder. She signs her name to the bill and hands it back. He pauses at the door.

"Will there be anything else?"

I turn when I hear the familiar buzzing voice. The room service guy is tall, with short black hair and dark eyebrows. Thick glasses make his eyes look large. Just before he closes the door behind him, he smiles at me and I see a flash of gold.

Marianne reaches under the room service cart and pulls out a duffel bag, struggling with its weight. "I think this is what you've been waiting for." She places it on the floor in front of Cal Ruderman.

He kneels and unzips it, dumps out stacks of bills in rubber bands.

"It's all hundreds in bundles of twenty-five grand," she says. "There are two hundred of them. It's all there. You can trust me."

"Sorry if I don't actually believe you." He paws through the cash. The goons circle. He hands a stack to each and they flip through it. After a few minutes, they seem satisfied. Banana Man stands and waves his crew toward him. "We'll assume it's all there." He smiles. "You know, honor among thieves."

Marianne turns her back on Banana Man. "You've got your money, just go." She walks toward me carrying two glasses of champagne.

For a moment, Banana Man seems ready to pounce on her, to go back on his part of the agreement and just do what he wants. Then he nods at the goons and they walk out of the room. The door clicks behind them.

"And take your damn fruit with you." Marianne takes a banana from the fruit basket and throws it. It hits the door, and the banana splits open, sliding down like a slug.

Marianne turns and clinks her glass with mine. "To you. For

grace under extreme pressure. Your boring lecture stalled him just long enough."

We drink.

"Long enough for what? For more of Ray's handiwork to show up?"

Marianne shakes her head. "Nope, it's the real stuff. Five million in hard-guy money, straight from New York."

"Are you going to explain or just keep it a mystery?"

There's a loud knock. We quit smiling and stare at the door, expecting Cal Ruderman to come crashing back through it.

"Room service."

I open the door and the room service guy jumps inside, pulls off his glasses, wrenches off his blue uniform jacket and throws it on the floor. "Uncle Ross! It's me! Good disguise, huh?"

Cray throws his arms around me and half-hugs, half-wrestles me across the room. Champagne sloshes on the carpet.

"That was incredible, Uncle Ross, really top-quality steaming bullshit."

"What are you talking about?"

"All that stuff about commodities and shit. I was listening outside the door and almost lost it a couple of times."

"I actually meant all of it," I say. "Except the part about democracy and freedom. That was over the top."

"Wow, you really are weirder than Dad," he says. "Because that was one out-there little Econ 101 riff. Like Alan Greenspan on acid. I figured you were just buying a little time until I showed up."

Marianne walks over and pulls off one of Cray's eyebrows.

"Ouch. How come you're always hurting me?"

She pulls off the other fake eyebrow and tosses it on the carpet. "That's for waiting outside the door listening. You should have knocked earlier. Those guys were about to start slicing."

"Uncle Ross was doing fine. Plus, I didn't want to show up too early and ruin the suspense."

Marianne leans forward. "The suspense?"

"I mean, weren't you kind of wondering whether I was going to show up at all? I drove straight from Vermont to New York, met with Malcolm, then drove here. Plus I had to buy a bottle of champagne and all the other props." He points at the room service tray.

"All I can say is we got incredibly lucky." Marianne refills my glass and hands one to Cray. We clink and drink. My legs are shaking. I sit down in a wingback chair.

"*Gak.*" Cray sprays champagne out of his nose, then scurries over to the minibar, comes back with an Amstel Light. He twists off the lid and drinks deeply.

"I still don't understand where you got the cash," I say. "And what's Malcolm got to do with it?"

Marianne walks over and puts her hands on my neck. "Good questions. All will be revealed."

I shake my head.

"We'll have plenty of time to clue you in on the details when we're on the road." Cray holds up his right hand. "Hey! Look what I found, Uncle Ross."

He's holding the DMK.

"I thought you lost that during your orthodontist appointment with the Cincinnati Police."

He shakes his head. "Had it in my pocket the whole time. I was just a little out of it, you know. On account of getting the shit pounded out of me. Anyway, guess what I have waiting outside?"

"A Chevy Scrotum?" I say.

Marianne shoots me a look.

"It's an uncle-nephew thing," Cray explains. "You wouldn't understand."

"Oh," she says.

"Anyway, there's a fine-looking 7-Series sedan waiting for us downstairs. Pack up, we got to fly this love nest slash crime scene."

"Wait a minute," I say. "Where're we going?"

near montpelier, vermont

We settle into our new day jobs, Marianne in the production department, me in proofing. After the initial excitement of our reunion wore off—about fifteen minutes, by my clock—my brother and I have fallen into our old roles. Ray is the devious boss. I am the silent helper and straight man with the fast fingers. Marianne becomes the beautiful coworker he's always trying to impress.

From my desk up in the loft, I catch Marianne's eye and wave. She smiles. Ray spots us.

"I really need that new paper over here, Marianne." At the center of the barn, Ray stands at the helm of the enormous

Heidelberg offset press, big as a truck. Marianne rolls over a cart loaded with paper and Ray docks it to the back of the press.

Ray hits a lever, the rollers start to spin, and the whole press starts to hiss like a dragon.

"This is a sheet-fed press," he shouts at Marianne. "At the Bureau of Engraving, they'd be running huge rolls of paper on a web press. But their runs are a lot longer, naturally." Though he left Chicago decades ago, somehow Ray's accent has deepened until he sounds like a ranting fry cook in some dump under the El.

Ray runs the barn like a squat, loudmouthed martinet. But as he reminds me constantly, he's saving our asses.

I watch Ray ink up the press, then send some paper running through it. He struggles to the other end and picks up the sheets, frowns at them, then tosses them into the burn can.

He resents printing $100 bills, the domain of any amateur with a color photocopier. It's like we've asked him to print the counterfeiting equivalent of *Moondance*, over and over. Five hundred thousand times, to be exact.

"What're you doing?" Marianne has left her post without permission and climbed up the stairs to my station.

"Getting rid of little pieces of dust." I point to the light board where the negative is lit from behind like a hospital X ray.

Marianne leans closer. "When's he actually going to start printing, Ross? We've been here for almost a month and he's still getting everything . . ." She raises two fingers on each hand for quotes. "Just right."

"Ray's annoying. And paranoid. And a perfectionist. But we really don't have a choice."

"I'm going to see if Malcolm will book us a couple of gigs in

Montpelier, or maybe over in Burlington," Marianne says. "There's got to be somewhere to play. The holidays are coming up. I haven't gone this long without a gig in years."

"We just have to deal with Ray for a couple of months," I say.

"Maybe we should have just let them cut your finger off," Marianne says.

I look up from covering a dust speck above Benjamin Franklin's head with opaque fluid.

"Kidding," she says. "Anyway, we have until New Year's Day to repay the Jersey boys."

Using her powers of persuasion, Marianne convinced Malcolm to connect her to a consortium of unnamed con men in New Jersey, who loaned her the $5 million in real cash to pay off the Banana Man. In return, we have to deliver $50 million in fake cash to a Paramus bar on January 1. The ten-to-one ratio seemed fair at the time, but now that we're in the trenches, printing money is starting to remind me of sorting peas.

Ray stands at the bottom of the ladder and tosses a printed page on the floor. "New proof!"

I sigh, stand up to retrieve the page.

There's a loud knock on the door.

"Lockdown!" Ray presses the button near the press and the burn can bursts into flame, destroying the evidence. Massive bolts click into place on the front and back doors.

Someone knocks again. Seven times, very loudly. "Hey! It's just me. I did the secret knock, Dad. Let me in, damn it. It's snowing out here."

Ray presses the button again and unlocks the door. Cray stumbles in, his parka hood bejeweled with ice.

"Where the hell have you been?"

"We stuck a mannequin in the snow in the middle of Route

12," Cray says. "Right near that new ski lodge place. Three Hummers in a pileup."

Ray rolls his eyes, pulls Cray close. "That's my boy."

Cray looks up, waves. "Hey Uncle Ross, Aunt Marianne." He's taken to calling Marianne this to annoy her. Or me. Or both of us. "Take a break for a minute. I got something to show you."

Marianne and I look at Ray. "Okay, okay. Take five. But no more."

Cray sheds his parka in a wet heap. He waves us over to the skinny ladder to his "office," the former cupola of the barn.

"The great thing about this place," he says as we climb the rickety ladder, "is that Dad's physically incapable of ever coming up here."

We nod. The idea of Ray on any ladder seems impossible. The cupola has windows on all four sides showing snow falling steadily over the low hills. The lights of Montpelier glow on the horizon, cut by the meandering black line of the Winooski River.

I can't imagine how the library table at the center of Cray's office ever got up here. But it is definitely never leaving. It's crowded with an ominous black computer, enormous flat-screen monitor, and all sorts of unidentifiable devices.

Cray slides into his chair and slumps down at the table, presses a few buttons to bring his electronic universe to life. Marianne and I stand behind him, holding hands the way young uncles and aunts do.

"You are going to totally dig this, Uncle Ross. I just got all the files back from the Japanese guy I'm collaborating with on *The Good Parts*."

"Your novel, right. I remember you telling me about it."

"My *novel*?" Cray looks up. "What century are you from?"

"This one. And the last one too, kind of."

Cray looks me in the eye. "I'm working on a next-level, multi-player interactive questing experience for gamers eighteen and over. In other words, a really dirty game that every fourteen-year-old will kill his grandmother to buy."

"Sounds great," Marianne deadpans. "And to think I killed grandma just to get Scrabble."

"Okay, now Aunt Marianne, promise not to get offended?"

Marianne nods. "Believe me, you're going to have to do a lot to offend me."

"Because most gamers are like, dudes." He hits a couple of keys. "Now remember, this is a rough compilation. We haven't put in all the backgrounds, all the sound, special effects, and most of the 3-D stuff." He turns off the dangling overhead light. "Here goes."

On the screen, I see a guy in a white shirt and black suit gliding down a city sidewalk. The familiar chords of *All Blues* emerge from Cray's speakers. "There are a bunch of choices for avatars," Cray says. "This guy is Miles."

A woman appears, coming toward us on the sidewalk. Cray hits a key and a list drops down on the side of the screen. "Here are your options."

I move closer, read the list. *Ask her to dinner. Buy her a drink. Steal her diamond. Have sex with her.* The list goes on. I close my eyes.

"Sound familiar, Uncle Ross? Anyway, you get points by gathering up things that have value." He clicks and a screen appears with icons—a diamond, a burrito, a six-pack of Amstel Light, wisdom (Socrates' bulbous head), money (stack of cash), power (Donald Trump's hair), freedom (Statue of Liberty torch).

I'm not sure whether to laugh or cry.

"This is all customizable, of course," Cray says. "Plenty of opportunities for product placement."

"Who decides what's valuable?" I ask.

"That, Uncle Ross, is a great question. This is no ordinary hunting and gathering game. You set the value on all your favorite things at the beginning and create—"

"A personal commodities market," I blurt out.

Cray shrugs. "I guess so. We're calling it a Values Profile. You can change it over time. You just gather up the things you decide are valuable and leave the rest of the shit alone. That's why the game's called *The Good Parts,* get it?"

"I get it," I say. "I really do."

"How do you win?" Marianne says.

"You kill all the other players," Cray says. "No, I'm kidding, Aunt Marianne. No one gets killed. Unless they get too much of one commodity. Then they max out and morph into two players."

"So there might be two guys named Miles out there, with one hunting for, say, diamonds, and the other hunting for burritos?"

Ross clicks his fingers. "That's right, Uncle Ross. Two or two hundred. Or two thousand. *The Good Parts* isn't about racking up points—there are armies of kids in Chinese click farms doing that all day. It's about figuring out what you like and then searching for it, like, relentlessly. Isn't that what life is all about?"

Marianne and I look at each other, stunned. There's too much right with what Cray's saying for us to disagree, too much wrong with it to nod blithely.

"Yes, exactly," Marianne says, finally. Now that she's seen Cray's home life, she's remarkably tolerant of him, feels sorry for him, even. "That's exactly what life's about, Cray."

Cray sends Miles sidling down the street again, winding between pedestrians, gathering items of value, passing along things he's done with, that he doesn't care about.

Cray clacks away at the keyboard, typing faster and faster, giggling at his own creation.

"We're about to do a press run!" Ray's shout echoes from downstairs but we don't pay much attention to it. Marianne and I take this stolen moment to look out over the frozen world, to pull closer and kiss.

Cray looks up from his computer. "Hey, get a room."

"We have a room," Marianne says. "It just isn't very nice."

Marianne and I are staying in what Ray calls his guest room, and if his guests were mushrooms, it would be fine. We've taken to reminiscing about hotel rooms with towels, heat, windows.

"So what do you think of it, Uncle Ross?"

"Of what?"

"*The Good Parts.*"

"I think you've found something pretty strange to spend your time on, Cray. And I mean that in a good way."

"I know you do. We're conferencing with a game packager in L.A. later this week. Any advice?"

"Get paid in advance," Marianne says.

"Get the contract in writing," I say. "Never go on a handshake."

"Don't give them anything extra."

"Don't bargain."

"Remember that people who hire you aren't your friends."

"Never drop your rate."

"You guys are brutal," Cray says. "Where'd you learn all that?"

"Somewhere out on the road," I say.

"What road, Uncle Ross?"

"The one that goes between nightclubs."

"Oh. I don't think I'm going to spend my life in nightclubs like you, Uncle Ross."

"Good to hear it," I say. "Warps your worldview."

Marianne reaches out and ruffles Cray's hair.

"Knock it off, Aunt Marianne." He bends away from her, his fingers never leaving the keyboard. He's connected to Tokyo, Beijing, San Francisco, New York. He's out there searching for the good parts, not just waiting for the ones that come his way.

"Press run!" Ray bellows from downstairs.

We should go back downstairs and help, but it's hard to leave Cray's rooftop shop and return to the grinding work of undermining the Bureau of Engraving. But we have Franklins to print before we sleep. Marianne and I watch the snow falling in orderly lines. Every now and then, a flake breaks free and traces an errant path, falling more slowly than the others.

I wonder what Miles Davis would think of all this. Then I realize that I don't really care. Miles has been dead for years.

"What are you guys going to do when we finally get all the money printed?" Cray asks.

I shrug. "Play some shows in New York."

"Maybe we'll get a new set together and head to Europe," Marianne says. "Good gigs in Germany."

"Or just see where the wind takes us."

"Press run!" Ray shouts from downstairs.

"Sounds like you guys don't have any more of an idea of what you're doing than I do," Cray says.

Marianne smiles. "We don't."

"And that's okay." I spent years at the keyboard, playing what people wanted to hear, what clubs paid me to play. It's time to search for the good parts.

Why rush the ending now?

acknowledgments

Special thanks to Karyn Marcus, John Schoenfelder, and Thomas Dunne Books for booking this novel's second act. Thanks also to Allan Guthrie, Jenny Brown Associates, Sharon Blackie, David Knowles, Matt Kennedy, Chris DeFrancesco, Ron Slate, Wesley Brown, Verena Wieloch, John Netzer, B. C. Krishna, Danny Spirer, Susan Dinsbier, and my family and friends.